MADE MEN VI

DRAGO

SARAH BRIANNE

YOUNG INK PRESS

Young Ink Press Publication
YoungInkPress.com

Edited by Hot Tree Editing and Diamond in the Rough Editing
Cover Art by Young Ink Press
Book design by Inkstain Design Studio
Text set in Centaur.

This work of fiction is intended for mature audiences only. All sexually active characters portrayed in this ebook are eighteen years of age or older. Please do not buy if sexual situations, violence, drugs, child abuse, and explicit language offends you.

Connect with Sarah:
AuthorSarahBrianne@gmail.com
www.facebook.com/AuthorSarahBrianne
@AuthorSarahBri

DRAGO

A MAN BY THE NAME OF...

For the last three months, blackness was all the man had known. Now, he was sure he had finally been delivered to Hell. He'd had it coming, and this was his purgatory.

For almost thirty years, he walked the earth as a merciless man. Now, as he walked this dark plane of nothingness, his soul only grew darker.

Repenting for his sins hadn't worked for him when he had been alive, and it definitely wasn't going to work for a man who was already in the pits of Hell.

"Delivery for Lucca Caruso. . ."

Something started to trickle into the darkness for the first time.

POP.

Grabbing his chest, he felt the explosive pain that had ceased his months of endless walking.

POP.

A strong sense of déjà vu told him this had happened to him before, back when he was alive.

POP.

He was reliving his death.

POP.

Even though his body had grown very weak here, his will refused to let him go down until…

POP.

Everything he had known, had grown used to over those lonely black days that turned into months, just disappeared. It was as if he entered a new plane, one that came with sounds and smells… and light. A plane that was beginning to seem all too familiar.

Dark lashes attached to heavy lids laid upon his sunken blue skin finally lifted, revealing his eyes. His pupils that were severely dilated slowly began to adjust to the light, turning his eyes from large black orbs to smaller pupils surrounded by brownish irises… Until the devilish red he had carried in them since birth appeared. The red that had given him his name. However, now that red flamed brighter, burning like a red ring of fire.

Eyes like that fit a dead man who had walked the bowels of Hell. Eyes that fit a dead man who had been spit out of Hell and brought back to life. Eyes that belonged to a man by the name of… Drago.

Some men just refused to fucking die.

Hell was a special place on earth, a place many people thought started six feet below the earth, but it didn't. Hell was exactly two thousand five hundred and fifty-six square feet, and she lived right in the fucking middle of it. It was a house that sat on the shitty side of Kansas City, Missouri, that she lived in practically her whole life. Almost eighteen long years she had been imprisoned here, and there was no knight in shining armor, let alone a god to save her. Those luxuries didn't exist for a girl like her.

Most people experienced their Heaven on earth only to greet Hell in death for the sins they'd committed. However, there were what she called the unlucky ones; the ones who weren't born like everyone else, pure and free of sin, but born into Hell itself. She was one of those unlucky ones.

All she knew was evil, fear, and hate. All four-letter words that had summed up her world since birth. Words and a world that she could never escape, except through death.

And it was all because of the blood that ran through her veins. A blood so wicked and disturbed it was like she could feel the coldness of it as it flowed through her body, so much so that it scared her shitless to think about what she could have become… or what she still could become.

When she looked up at herself in the mirror, it was as if she could see the monster that lay right under the surface, but it just hadn't been woken up yet. Staring into her eyes that her father had given her told her it was there… The big black orbs of abyss promised her there was evil inside of her too, no matter how much she told herself she was nothing like him.

You just weren't born the daughter of Lucifer without being fucking crazy.

SETTING HIS FATE IN STONE

D*o you know what it's* like to look in the mirror and not know who it is looking back at you? Staring at his reflection for the first time in months, he didn't recognize the man before him. He had always been big. In high school he didn't even pass as a student because he looked bigger than grown-ass men. Drago was called "the tank" because that's what he was: a fucking tank for the Caruso crime family. He practically had been born and bred to take and carry out any hit for the Family. Almost all the De Santis men were, but something about Drago De Santis had been special, making him the best bodyguard the Carusos ever had. Until now… His muscle mass… gone. Along with the man he once knew. His strength and size were what made him Drago, and without it, it was like he no longer deserved the name. Drago De Santis had been replaced by a weak stick of a man who wouldn't be capable of taking one bullet to the chest and live to tell the tale.

Lifting a tired hand to his gaunt face, he touched the beard that now graced his skin, then pushed back the long, shaggy black hair out of his eyes. It all made him look even more unrecognizable; he'd always had a clean-shaven face and kempt hair along with most of the men in the Caruso family.

Unable to hold the mirror the nurse had given him any longer, he slammed it down without much force. It was like his body had betrayed him, too weak to even hold a one-pound mirror, let alone get out of bed to take a piss. His body had fallen apart, and even after spending months at the gates of Hell, this was what was going to break him, 'cause at least there his body hadn't betrayed him.

"My father wasn't sure if you were going to make it." A voice sounded from the dim doorway to his hospital room.

His eyes trailed over to see the shadowy figure he knew all too well. "What do you want, Lucca?"

Walking into the room, the underboss took a seat in the chair that sat by the bed. "I know what you're trying to do, and it's not going to work."

Drago knew what he was referring to; he had told the nurses and the staff not to let anyone see him. Not wanting anyone seeing him pissing through a bag, but it was too late for that, and dumb of him to think Lucca wouldn't come see him after what happened. Swallowing hard, he finally looked his underboss in the eyes. "How is she?"

"We both know I wouldn't be here if she weren't okay," Lucca said coldly with a matter-of-fact edge.

Knowing he'd either be locked up behind bars or six feet under by now getting his retribution, Drago nodded his head with a sense of relief before saying the last words he needed to say, "I'm sorry I failed you."

"That's the last thing you did," he admitted before standing up to slip out the way he had come in.

"If your father saw me right now, he'd know I didn't make it," Drago confessed through a whisper before he could leave.

"No, you didn't." Fierce blue-green eyes turned back to stare him down for several seconds before he spoke again. "But the new Drago did."

It was in that moment he felt the fire begin somewhere deep inside of him. He looked down at his weak body; it was strange to see the outside not match the inside. "What if I can't come back from this?"

"You will for one reason." Lucca gave a slow smile of pure sin. "Revenge."

At that one final word, the flames grew brighter.

Revenge was a weird thing. You could seek revenge on one person your whole life, and when it finally struck, was all over, and didn't fix anything, you realized quickly it didn't solve the problem.

That six-letter word was the only thing she wanted her father to finally meet, and now the devil was dead and gone. She hadn't personally taken her revenge out on him, but the Carusos had, and she and her brothers all reveled in it. She didn't think that if she swung the sword and had been the one to personally do it, she would feel differently about revenge. But she supposed the only one who knew that was the man who had swung it.

Was she glad he'd swung it even if revenge wasn't really that sweet?...

. . .Hearing the front doorknob jingle, her ten-year-old lanky body jumped up from the couch she was sitting on beside her twin brothers. Knowing it was all too late, she stood frozen as she looked at the big brown door, waiting for death to walk through. When hands covered the door, blocking it from opening, her eyes met her older brother's brave ones.

Dominic mouthed the word "Go" as he strongly kept the door held.

She quickly made a run for it with one final look at her brother, hoping it wouldn't be the last time.

"What the fuck!" The yelling started on the other side. "Open this damn door! I'm going to fucking kill...."

The farther she ran, the less she could hear, until she flung the door to the basement open and shut it behind her. She was sliding her back down the door, the tears slipping down her cheeks as she held her hand over her mouth, trying to cry as quietly as possible.

It wouldn't matter how loud she cried. The beating she could hear on the other side of the door was loud enough to drown her out. It was just a habit. . .

...Yes, she fucking was.

"Come in, Drago."

Walking through the office door to see Lucca sitting with Dante and Vinny took him by surprise, as he wasn't expecting the boss and the consigliere. It had taken one fucking long month to even be able to walk to take a seat in front of them, let alone the bit of muscle he was beginning to build back again. He wasn't close to a hundred percent yet and definitely wasn't as big as he used to be, but every day he got closer and closer. His recovery was a hard road, and it wasn't over yet, but just like his underboss had predicted, the thought of getting revenge against the family who'd almost sent him to his grave was what gave him his miraculous speedy recovery since awakening.

Expecting Dante or Lucca to tell him why he was called in, he was surprised again it was actually Vinny who spoke. "While you were in a coma, I made a suggestion in order to bring long-term peace between the two families, and both Dante and Dominic agreed."

The hairs stood up on Drago's back. By now he'd been told everything that went down about the meeting between them and the Luciano brothers while he was out, but he was beginning to figure out that they left out an important part of the deal.

Lucca reached for a cigarette, then flicked his Zippo open quickly to light the end as he took a long, deep hit.

Fuck, they did.

"It was agreed that we would pick a woman from the Luciano family to wed a Caruso. So blood could mix and trust could be earned once again."

The feeling of dread washed over him.

Their consigliere continued setting his fate in stone. "And we all agreed on you."

"What?!" Was he hearing them fucking right? "You can't be serious."

Three silent men met his eyes, showing just how serious they were.

His mouth went dry. "Absolutely not. I am not marrying a fucking Luciano!"

Again, no one sympathized.

Frustrated, he stood up. Keeping his voice calm, he spoke each word clearly. "They almost fucking killed me, and you expect me to marry one?"

The cigarette he had just lit hit the ashtray as Lucca smashed it deep into the glass, suffocating the fire. A small trail of smoke floated into the air, it all just showing exactly how fucking serious he was. "I do."

"Is this an order?" he asked, the words coming out slowly. Looking back at the man he had gotten closer to, he would almost call that psychopath his friend. It was him he looked at for the answer, his underboss, even with his boss in this very same room.

It was Dante who answered angrily from the disrespect. "It's a Goddamn order."

Flexing his jaw, he waited for Lucca to save him from his fate in some way, but he never did. Knowing him, it was probably his sick idea. He took calming breaths for several minutes, coming to the conclusion there was nothing he could do as clearly their minds were made up. No Caruso, let alone a De Santis, denied an order from the boss unless they wanted to lose a finger. He figured they had picked him because he was a De Santis, one of the most loyal members in the family since the mob had been formed. Not to mention his personal status within the family being the boss's personal bodyguard. His age of twenty-nine with no woman in sight of possibly marrying one day probably sealed the deal. No matter how much he didn't want this, he did understand it in a fucked-up way, and if the roles were reversed, he would have made the same decision.

So, nodding his head, he bit the bullet, giving the approval they didn't even need. The mafia hadn't had an arranged marriage in a long time, and he believed he was going to be the first one in the twenty-first century.

"Glad you could see it our way." Vinny smiled.

Like I had a fucking choice. Quickly, he began to realize something else... "Who did you pick for me to marry?"

Dante's ice-blue eyes glowed. "We realize this is a lot for us to ask of you, so we are giving you the choice."

"Hmm." Leaning back in his seat, he was almost tickled. Drago should have known it would be his boss to take care of him. He supposed he could deal with that. He would pick the hottest one with the least amount of ties to that fucking family, fuck her every now and then, and continue on with his life and make his bosses happy. It didn't matter much, anyway; he'd never wanted to get married, so it wasn't like he was losing out on finding the woman he wanted to spend the rest of his life with. That shit didn't exist for him. "When do I get to choose?"

"They are ready for us to come today," Lucca answered with a thin air of smoke escaping from the new cigarette he'd just lit.

He clapped his hands together, ready. "Line 'em up."

There was something Drago missed, however, what he completely overlooked. The slight smile… that held Lucca's lips.

I BEG OF YOU

D*rago walked down the line* of the Luciano women who were lined up perfectly in a row. Each one was different to the next, giving him many options, but none of them had sparked an interest in him so far. He reached the last one in the row; she was easily the hottest one in the bunch. The right age, the right face, and the right fucking body. Hell, the bitch was practically asking to get picked the way her red bra and big tits popped out of her shirt, not to mention the way she kept eye fucking him.

Smiling, he could just imagine how pissed the Lucianos would be to take her ass away from them. This was the day he had been waiting for since the bullets had ripped through his body. *Payback's a bitch.* Opening his mouth, he had finally made his decision. "She'll d—"

"This is all your women?" Lucca asked from the corner of the room, stopping him from sealing the deal.

The room went dead silent, till a throat was cleared and a deep voice escaped the oldest Luciano brother. "Yes."

"Don't lie to me, Dominic," he warned with a deadly whisper as he stepped away from the corner till he stood inches away.

Squaring his shoulders, the new Luciano boss looked him straight in his eyes. "These are all the Luciano women over the age of eighteen. Just like we promised."

"All right." Lucca raised a brow. "Then you don't mind if I look around, do you?"

There was a slight flex in his jaw. "Not at all."

As he left the room, Lucca's shoulder pushed into Dominic's as he passed by, before he disappeared into the Luciano home.

Wondering what the fuck his underboss was up to, Drago decided to let it play out, even though his decision was made. His eyes moved over the men in the room while they waited for Lucca's return. There seemed to be a silent shift, his protective instincts going on high alert. He looked at Dominic first. It was his teeth he ground just a bit too tightly; he was almost undetectable. Then to the middle brother, Matthias, who was the most obvious. His leg bounced up and down harder and harder with every minute that passed while sitting in the chair he was slouched in. The Caruso's were holding his identical twin, Angel, as collateral for the time being, so he supposed he had more to lose if this deal went bad. The last brother, Cassius, however, was very young and in the early stages of high school. There was something about that kid Drago didn't like. He reminded him of those kids in the horror movies who were possessed and stared at you a little bit too long. He was a scary little fucker with obscure eyes who definitely had no business being here. *Fucking Lucianos.*

A few more minutes passed till they could hear footsteps coming back toward them. Lucca entered the room again, and it wasn't till he took a step toward the right did he reveal who he found.

Drago stared at the young woman standing behind him. She was pale with long hair that looked almost blond but wasn't; it was the lightest shade of pink he'd ever seen. Her eyes, however, were as black as the leather jacket and eye makeup she wore. It all made her look even paler than she probably was.

"Fuck." Matthias jumped up from his seat.

Dominic took a step toward her, trying to grab her. "S-She's only seventee—"

A hand came up, silencing him. Turning, Lucca stared the girl down, addressing her. "Is that so?"

Her black orbs danced between the three Luciano brothers.

"I'd advise you not to lie or"—his finger came out to touch her chin lightly to make her finally look at him—"your *brothers,*" he emphasized, letting the room know he knew exactly who she was, "are going to find out the hard way to never fucking lie to me again."

You could hear a pin drop in the room from the deafening silence. The only thing that rivaled the quietness was the tension.

She swallowed hard as the truth came out. "I'm eighteen."

Vinny's voice filled the silence with a hard consigliere tone. "I'd advise you and your men not to lie to the Caruso family, Dominic. I thought by us keeping Angel in our possession, that was understood."

Understanding the threat he was just given, he held the bridge of his nose, clearly trying to think of how to get out of this fucking mess. "She's my—*our*—only sister, Lucca, and she is only safe here with us. Please, you have a sister. I beg of you to try to understand."

Looking at her a moment longer, Lucca dropped his finger. "Get in line," he hissed fatally at her.

Drago watched her bravely walk to stand beside the woman he had already chosen.

"Now, you may choose," his underboss gave him the order.

He walked the line once more, this time paying close attention to each prospect, making it all the way down to the woman he was seconds away from choosing. Truthfully, it was his dick that wanted to pick her. The way she eye fucked him now as she licked her lips made the decision even easier. However, there was a desperation in her eyes he had overlooked the first time. She was simply the decoy to keep him distracted; he saw that now. The Lucianos so clearly wanted him to pick her, knew she would be too irresistible not to choose. *And I took the bait…* Taking a final step, he stood in front of the pretty pink-haired girl… *Almost.*

Drago lifted his fingers, and unlike Lucca, he grabbed her chin, holding it tightly between his finger and thumb to force her eyes to his. "What's your name, sweetheart?"

"Katarina." Her voice came out huskier than he would have thought was possible for her age. "Katarina Luciano."

He stared down at her. She sure as fuck wasn't what he wanted. She was far too young for his taste and was definitely not his type, wearing too dark eye makeup and leather. He preferred a more natural look. She not only fit the Luciano esthetic of a rougher vibe, but she looked like a Luciano, not to mention she fucking *was* one. The worst kind. Three words were whispering through his mind over and over as he continued to stare at her. *The devil's daughter.*

Drago had been close to choosing with his dick, but now something much more satisfying was going to decide who it was he was going to marry, and it was going to taste so sweet. Dropping his hand from the tiny chin, he looked over at his underboss, the slight smile visible to him finally. *You really are a sick fuck.*

Unable to stop himself from glancing at her once more, he let himself do so only for a split second before he looked back at Lucca. Quickly, he nodded, giving his final decision to his underboss before he turned to walk out.

"What does that mean?" Cassius asked, raising his voice louder when the solemn room didn't answer. "What does that fuckin' mean?!"

Matthias was the one to grab his little brother up to keep them from all getting killed.

Drago didn't look back. The bullets the Lucianos had driven deep into his heart had killed it. He made his decision the second he saw her devil eyes, and the ruin he was going to cause that fucking family might finally give him a full night's rest since he'd been at the gates of Hell.

Payback wasn't a bitch. It was a fucking monster.

If you thought this was going to be a love story where they fall in love the second their eyes met… you were wrong. This isn't it.

LOVE A LUCIANO

"*Wouldn't he like to go* out on a date with Katarina or one of the others before he chooses?" Dominic was scrambling.

"He has made his decision," Vinny said.

Katarina stood there, shell-shocked, staring blankly in front of her, where the man she might soon be calling her husband stood. He had only looked at her for mere seconds before he nodded his head, then disappeared from the room. And just like that her whole life was supposed to fucking change.

"What is the rush? It's not like they have to get married right this second."

"No, but we expect a marriage by the end of the month."

END OF THE MONTH??

"For fuck's sake." Dominic watched as Vinny and Lucca walked toward the door. He tried one more time. "Lucca, please." He grabbed his arm, stopping the Caruso underboss knowing very well doing so could end his life. Looking into his eyes, he pleaded, "I'm only asking for them to spend one day together. That's it."

Lucca was silent for several moments, as if he was contemplating several different ways to kill him, before he finally answered with a slight tilt to his lips. "One day, Dominic. That's it."

"Thank you." A huge sigh of relief escaped him as he let him go. "Thank you."

The Carusos left with a few final words from Vinny. "We will be in touch."

Hearing the door slam should have knocked her out of her shocked trance, but it didn't. Instead, she kept staring straight forward, replaying the images of him choosing her again and again.

"He picked Kat, didn't he?" Cassius asked solemnly.

Finally letting him go, Matthias confirmed by nodding his head.

"Get out!" Dominic roared to the women who were in the room before they all quickly scattered out the door.

The youngest brother vowed, "We can't let them get away with this."

"We're not." Dominic came over to Katarina, placing his hands on her shoulders. "You're not—" He stared down into her black depths. "—I don't give a fuck what you do on that day you spend with him, but you be the biggest fucking pain in the ass he has ever dealt with. Make him not want to fucking look at you a moment longer, make being around you unbearable. Be the motherfucking biggest bitch there ever was and make him fuckin' regret wanting to pick you, Kat."

Her other two brothers came to stand beside them, both nodding their heads in agreement.

"You don't get it," she whispered as her eyes turned glossy. They didn't see it, couldn't see it. "He hated me the second he saw me because he knew exactly who I was. There is nothing I can do that will make him hate me any more than he already does, and nothing is going to change his mind from marrying me because... this is his revenge."

It was hard for the last words to come out, but they all knew who Drago was, the man their father had almost killed. Since Drago's fall and Chloe's capture, the Lucianos came under new order by her oldest brother, Dominic, after Lucca killed her father, Lucifer. Her marrying a Caruso would insure the Lucianos' loyalty forever. And not only that, but it would break apart the very family Drago despised with all his being.

She had seen that look in a man's eyes before as they'd looked at her, one of pure hatred. It never burned or hurt any less than the hundreds of times before. It was something only one of her brothers understood, and that brother wasn't here.

Dropping his hands from her shoulders, he stood up straight, commanding not only her attention but his brothers' with a tone so fierce it could only be matched by a god. "Katarina, you are a Luciano, and a Luciano never rolls over to die. We fucking fight like hell."

Looking out the house window, she saw the big black Cadillac Escalade pull up.

"It's time," Matthias told her with sadness in his voice.

Taking a deep breath, she headed for the door

"Kat...."

Turning, she looked at the half of the twin set who remained in the Luciano household.

"If you see *him,* you tell him we haven't forgotten about him and that here,"—he pointed to the old creaky floor beneath his feet—"this is his home."

She nodded her head seeing the toll being separated from his other half had taken on him since Angel had been taken away from them. Matthias and Angel had been inseparable since inception, two perfectly identical twins who even marred their bodies identically. Tattooing images on their bodies from head to toe that were as identical as them. The only difference were the sides they marked, becoming perfect mirror images of each other. However, that was the outside; what they were on the inside couldn't be more opposite than the sun and the moon.

As she went out the door, Dominic was waiting on the other side watching a man exit the dark-tinted Escalade and opening the back door for her to enter. She took a step not wanting to drag out the day any longer, but her brother, the new boss of the Luciano family, wouldn't let her leave without a final request.

"Give him hell."

She felt sorry for him, for Matthias, and for Cassius. They had false hope, hope that would come crashing down on him the day she would have to walk down that aisle.

Sliding into the car, with it being so dark inside, she had missed him at first. It wasn't until the door closed and the darkness encapsulated them that she saw him sitting in the seat on the other side.

"Angel!" She jumped halfway out of her seat to hug the twin brother she hadn't seen in what seemed like forever. "You have to go inside real quick. Matthias would love—"

Angel sat there shaking his head while the other Caruso got back into the car.

"But…." When the driver started the car and began to leave the lot, the confusion quickly went away and pain struck her heart. She supposed he wasn't allowed that privilege by the Carusos, but that wasn't what hurt. It was the disappointment that wasn't there on his face from not being able to go in and see his family. The scary thing was, Angel could see that she knew it too.

This made the car ride solemnly quiet, especially with the presence of the Caruso men in the car, and it wasn't until they pulled up to the most beautiful home she had ever seen that the silence disappeared.

"I need a minute with my sister."

Surprised when the men left the car and closed them into privacy, she looked over at her brother.

"How are you feeling?" he asked with deeply hidden worry in his voice.

She hadn't even realized how she had been holding in her breath since they pulled up. Finally, she let the air out. "Like I'm going to throw up."

"You're going to be fine." He took her shaking hand, griping it hard.

"Yeah, well, if I throw up, I'll just aim for him. That's what Dom says to do, anyway. He wants me to be a pain in his ass."

"Kat, I need you to listen to me."

Suddenly, the grip on her hand became harder.

"That's not going to scare him away from choosing you. That's only going to solidify his choice."

Her head fell. "I know." She knew Angel would be the only one to understand when someone looked at you with pure hatred, and how that person seeing you in not only sadness but anger gave them exactly what they wanted.

He squeezed her hand a little tighter, the worry in his voice now turned to deep sadness, "You have to get him to fall in love with you, Katarina."

"W-What?" She looked up at her brother seeing the sadness not only in his voice but marred on his face.

"The only way to scare him into not choosing you is by scaring him into thinking he could love a Luciano." Angel's voice descended to almost a whisper. "Trust me, I would know."

She had heard the rumors of Angel getting close to a Caruso girl but couldn't believe it till she could see it with her own eyes, and now… she had. That difference in him she had spotted almost immediately was him changing. Whereas Matthias was falling apart without his twin, Angel was thriving.

The Carusos were beginning to suit him, literally down to the tailored suit that gripped his body, like the Carusos had a grip on him. She wondered if they weren't holding him here against his will.

Would you even run?

Letting her hand drop from his, she placed her hand on the door to open it, but she stopped herself from doing so for just a moment. "You know he's dying without you..." When the quiet car somehow grew quieter even with her voice filling it, she continued. "Matthias isn't like the rest of us, you know? We're monsters. And unlike you, he's the angel." Throwing open the door, she had to fight back the tear that wanted to fall. "Lucifer just broke his fucking wings."

I'LL BE DAMNED

Knock. Knock.

She felt fire rise in the pit of her belly when Angel knocked on the door they now stood in front of, and when the door flew open to a clearly annoyed dragon-eyed man, the fire pit in her stomach blazed brighter.

Drago simply just stood to the side, going to let her enter without saying a word.

Swallowing hard, she took a step into the home, passing the tall Caruso bodyguard.

"Not you, Luciano," he spat, placing a hand on Angel's chest, keeping him from entering. "I can take it from here."

She turned around quickly to see Angel mouth the words *Good luck* before the door was closed in his face. That was when she realized maybe she'd judged her brother too quickly, and that he just might run if he had been given a chance.

Then, just like that, she was alone, *with him.* An eerie feeling she was clearly going to have to get used to. When he started walking her through the huge foyer that held a wrought iron staircase, her eyebrows drew together. "Is this your home?" she asked. The words just simply fell out. This wasn't exactly what she'd expected to walk into; this place was gigantic, modern, and breathtaking. Not exactly the bachelor pad she had expected him to have.

He thankfully didn't take offence and answered frankly. "No, this is the Caruso family home where my boss and his children live. I have a room here, since I'm here a lot of the time."

"Oh." She wondered how that would work if they did get married, and if so, where she would end up staying. Being a Luciano, her best guess certainly wasn't fucking here.

When they walked into the living and kitchen area, she was even more in awe as he continued talking.

"I have to finish some stuff up here first, but Lucca thought you might be more comfortable here for a bit."

"All right." She supposed, unsure of what to do next in the hell of an awkward situation she was in.

"Maria? Maria!" A young boy came from the foyer carrying a textbook. "Do you know where Maria is?" he asked Drago when he entered the living space.

"I don't know where her crazy ass is," he answered gruffly.

"Well, I need her help with my math."

Seeing the cute boy stressed, she found words falling out of her mouth yet again. "Would you like me to see if I can help you?"

"Sure." He shrugged with a wicked smile when he finally noticed her and practically ran to the couch.

She looked at Drago to see if it was okay. He seemed a bit shocked that she offered, but he didn't protest her into not helping him. So, she followed the kid to the couch with a smile assuming this was probably what Lucca had meant by being more comfortable here.

"I'm Leo." He held out a strong hand when she reached the couch.

"I'm Katarina, but you can call me Kat if you want." She took his hand, shaking it, unable to get the smile off her face. Whoever this kid was had some serious women skills already. A few more years, and he was going to be a lady killer.

"Kat," he repeated, sticking her name in his head. "Your hair is sick."

"Thanks." She laughed knowing it was a compliment. "Now, let's see if I can help you."

He opened the book as she sat down next to him and pointed to the problem he was stuck on in his homework.

"My brother Cassius is learning this in school too." Her assumption of him being around her brother's age had been right. She took his pencil and paper, writing out the problem. Out of the corner of her eye she saw Drago just standing there staring, which was making her feel self-conscious, but finally, he left the room, which let her work out the problem easier as she began trying to teach Leo.

However, they only had worked out half the problem when she

saw Drago return with a bunch of paperwork and take a seat at the end of the kitchen table, keeping them in his view. It took a while for her to begin to forget about him again, and by the time they were toward the end of the problems, someone started coming from the foyer again. When she looked at who it was, her jaw practically dropped to the floor when a tall blond model entered the room.

"Where were you?" Drago was the one to ask.

"What do you care?" She laughed as she went to sit on the couch. Rolling her eyes when his face became serious, she answered. "I was in my bedroom on the phone."

"I thought you looked for her?" he asked, giving Leo a stern look.

"She must've not heard me when I knocked." Leo shrugged.

"You should have knocked harder then."

"It's okay," she interjected, noticing Drago getting a little frustrated. "I don't mind helping him. We're already almost done."

"Thank God. If I have to teach him PEMDAS one more time, I'm going to shoot myself." The woman touched by Jesus himself smiled at her. "I'm Maria."

Smiling back, she figured the woman was definitely Leo's older sister. "Katarina."

"You can call her Kat though," Leo added.

"Your hair is freaking gorgeous," Maria complimented her, looking at the light pink strands.

"Thank you." Hearing a shuffle of papers, she noticed Drago stand up and beginning to pack up his papers, but she turned back to Leo. "Ready to finish?"'

"Do I have to? It's not like I'm going to use this when I'm done with high school."

Even though she had heard that typical response from every other teenager, she had gotten a different vibe from the kid since he was the one who'd sought help. "How do you know?"

Leo smiled proudly. "Because I'm going to be like my brother Lucca, one day."

Huh.... "Lucca's your brother?"

"Yeah." Maria was the one to answer, seeming to be dumbfounded by her response.

"Oh." She licked her dry lips seeing that even Drago had stopped packing up. "I don't see the resemblance, is all. You two are very..." Katarina tried to search for the right word. "...good looking."

Maria's jaw dropped. "You don't think Lucca's good looking?"

Oh fuck. She stared at the shocked faces in the room thinking she had just made a huge mistake telling them she didn't find not only their brother handsome but the Caruso underboss. However, she couldn't help it. She really didn't find him attractive at all. He was quite fucking frightening to her. Wondering if she should try to backtrack, she decided to fuck it and just be truthful. "Not really, no."

"What?!" The sister's voice came out half shocked but filled with laughter. "Every girl he meets falls in love with him."

How in the hell? Now she was the one with a shockingly pain-struck face. "Really?"

"YES." Maria continued to die with laughter realizing she was being serious in not finding him attractive.

Drago placed his papers on the table and sat back down again.

Shrugging, she had to make sure and try to reel it back. This was the underboss, for Christ's sake. "He's just not my type, I guess."

"Then what's your type?" Leo asked with an arched brow.

Handing the pencil for him to solve the last problem, she answered him truthfully. "Men who are smart."

Leo couldn't have grabbed the pencil any faster.

Katarina wasn't sure if she heard the mumble coming from Drago's direction correctly over Maria's even louder hilarity, but she could have sworn she heard the words….

"I'll be damned."

HE'S AN IDIOT

"*Can we get pizza?*"

"Leo!" Maria hissed at him.

"Sorry, I forgot." His voice trailed off.

She was confused at first as to why she had hushed him, but then she quickly remembered her brother telling her how Lucifer had taken down Drago. Posing as a pizza delivery guy had gotten Drago to open the door and make an almost fatal mistake.

Drago didn't even look up from his work. "I'll get one of the guys to bring some pizza."

She figured the Carusos had unfortunately learned their lesson. Hence why she was here. It was all going very differently than she anticipated, not knowing what she had expected, but it wasn't this. Katarina wasn't even really spending the day with Drago per say, but she figured he wanted it that way, distancing her from himself, so his mind wouldn't change. She had barely learned anything new about him; the only things she did know about him were what Dominic had told her—that she needed to know everything she could about the enemy in order to defeat him. In order to get him to change his mind in choosing her. She learned Drago De Santis was the boss' personal bodyguard and one of the most respected men in the family, like most De Santis men were. The night he had been taken down, he was here, in the Caruso family home, when he was shot and the woman he was protecting, Chloe, was captured. All she knew of Chloe was that her father had been fascinated with her and to stay the hell away from her, as she was Lucca's.

When there was a knock on door, Drago went to open it, and Leo excitedly went to the kitchen to grab a seat at the counter while Maria followed her brother. She was following behind them but stopped when she saw Drago just standing in the foyer staring at the door.

Her feet stepped almost unknowingly toward him. When she reached him, it was like she was seeing him for the first time. Without a barrier between them. For a moment, it had been brought down, and you could see… pain.

Going to the door, she did what he couldn't find himself to do, open it.

"Who are you?" A guy in a suit smiled perfectly but seemed to be surprised to see someone other than Drago open it.

Smiling back, she took the pizzas from the handsome blond.

"I'm Ka—"

Thud.

Blinking at the fact that Drago just slammed the door in his face, she couldn't believe he did that. "Was that one of your men?"

"Yes."

"Then why did you slam the door in his face?" *He was kinda cute.*

"Because he's an idiot," he said, simply taking the pizzas from her.

Okay, so, so far, she had learned he didn't particularly like anyone. She noticed he didn't like Maria, he really didn't like that blond guy, and even Leo seemed to get on his nerves a bit. She wondered who exactly he did like, if anyone.

Turning to head back, she was stopped in her tracks when she saw a girl standing close to the bottom of the stairs. She was breathtakingly beautiful with long black hair and light skin that was as pale as her gray eyes. She knew exactly who she was, and it wasn't the scar that marked the side of her face that gave it away. It was the nightmares that were hidden behind her eyes.

"Hi." Another word fell out of her mouth, knowing good and well she should have kept walking, and when Drago slightly took a step forward and stood between them, she realized she probably really should have.

Clasping her hands tightly together, the girl managed to get the word out. "H-Hi."

A sweet expression appeared on her face along with her tone. "I'm Kat."

"C-Chloe."

She had confirmed what she knew before she'd spoken her name. It was like she knew her, understood her, all in a single glance. Probably better than anyone else.

"We have pizza. You should come eat with us." Katarina smiled before walking to the kitchen, not wanting to place any pressure on the girl. Shockingly, she followed, coming into the kitchen as she placed the pizzas on the counter.

"Hey, Chloe," Leo and Maria greeted her just as sweetly as she had.

Instantly, she got more comfortable seeing them. "Hey."

"How did your test go?" Maria asked, revealing she must have online classes in what she would assume to be college.

"Pretty good."

"Good. Now, let's eat." The young brother started ripping open the pizza boxes.

She found it strange when they all grabbed a plate from the counter but Drago. She watched him go to the fridge to grab a protein shake, then headed back to his table to work. Placing a big slice of pizza on her plate, she bit her lip before taking a seat at the counter.

You have to get him to fall in love with you, Katarina, Angel's voice whispered through her mind. Even though it scared her to death, she headed toward Drago, knowing Angel was the brother with the right advice.

Putting her plate on the table beside his papers, she sat down next to the man who didn't even look over at her when she did.

"You don't want any pizza?" she asked, being sure to be polite.

"I can grab you a slice if you wan—"

"If I did, I would have grabbed my own," he cut her off.

Fine. She picked up her pizza and took a huge bite out of it. The man clearly had no taste if he could scarf down that gross-looking protein shake like that.

Continuing to eat, she couldn't care less what he was staring intently at, but Katarina had a problem of being nosy where numbers were concerned. And he was definitely writing the wrong number down. "Two thousand and forty-one."

"Excuse me?" Finally, he looked up at her.

"It's two thousand and forty-one dollars, not two thousand and thirty-one."

The look on his face showed he clearly didn't believe her, so he punched the numbers in the calculator again and quickly, his face changed. "Oh. I must have punched it wrong in the calculator."

"Mistakes happen." She shrugged taking another huge bite, but she was unable to keep her eyes from straying. "The one before is wrong too. Should be five thousand six hundred and seventy-five dollars and seventy-eight cents."

"For fuck's sake," he mumbled under his breath.

"Lucca usually does payroll, but he's been trying," Maria told her with a snicker as she came to sit down beside her with a slice of pizza.

"You two need to mind your fucking business and leave me alone. You shouldn't even be looking at this."

Leo joined them, bringing a whole pizza box with him to see what they were arguing about.

"Christ!" Drago started packing up the papers.

"Third one down should be a seven, not an eight."

He grabbed the bridge of his nose. "Fucking hell."

"Is she right?" Leo asked with a mouth full of pizza.

Even Chloe came over with her pizza to see what he was going to say as he started punching the numbers in.

The eraser hitting the paper was their answer.

Maria's cackling filled the space.

Drago, however, put down the pencil and stared intently at her. "What's a thousand four hundred and forty-five times eight?"

Swallowing the pizza, she gave him the answer. "Eleven thousand five hundred and sixty."

It was Maria who grabbed the calculator from him to see if she was right. "Holy shi—"

"Whoa!" Leo dropped his pizza, so impressed that he wanted to see her do it again. "What's five hundred and six divided by twelve?"

"Forty-two point one seven."

The blond punched it in the calculator. "She's right again."

Even Chloe was fascinated. "W-What about nine hundred and eighty-seven dived by three hundred and nine?"

"Three point one nine."

Leo was the one to snatch the calculator from his sister's hand, putting it in. "This is so cool! She's like a human calculator."

"I suppose." She shrugged before looking at Drago, whose eyes hadn't left her. "Here." Leaning over, she took the payroll paper, placing another paper over the names to cover them before grabbing a paperclip off another set of papers to hold it in place. That way she could do it for him quickly, and he wouldn't worry about her seeing the names. Katarina couldn't care less who got paid what; she just couldn't watch him continuing to butcher the math. "May I?" she asked, holding out her hand for the pencil that was just out of reach.

He stared at her harder for a second longer. This time, they looked a lot like hers did when she'd felt like she was seeing him for the first time just minutes ago. Except this time… he was seeing her. Picking the pencil back up, he placed it in her much smaller hand.

His fingertips grazed her palm. She wondered if they stayed there for just a little too long. *Is it working?* Katarina smiled sweetly at him.

Looking over at Leo, she raised a brow. "Wanna time me to see how long it takes?"

"Heck yes." He pulled his phone out of his pocket. "One… two…"

Cracking her knuckles and getting her pencil ready, she couldn't help but notice the smile behind those strange ring-of-fire eyes.

"Three…."

It's working.

"Go!"

DRAGO'S GIRLFRIEND

S*omehow, she, along with everyone* else, ended up in an Escalade, and before she knew it, they were in front of the Kansas City Casino Hotel that was owned by the Caruso boss.

When Drago parked, Leo got out of the SUV quickly, opening it for them. Chloe, who was in the third row, got up to get out first but paused when Leo held out a hand.

Katarina only saw her pause for a split second, and even though she could get out of her side of the door like Maria did out of the passenger side, she instinctively scooted out the back seat taking Leo's hand in hers. "Thanks, Leo."

"No problem." The young teen shook his head, clearly remembering something. This time when Chloe got out, he just held the door open without giving her his hand.

"T-Thank you."

Walking toward the door, she could see confused looks on Maria's and Drago's face while they looked at her.

"How'd she. . . ." Maria's voice trailed off when Chloe came closer.

It was Leo who opened all the doors and led the girls into the huge casino and pressing the button for the elevator while Drago followed close behind.

Katarina couldn't help but think how sweet Leo was, Lucca's brother, knowing full well he would never be like his older brother despite his hopes.

With all of them getting into the elevator, she found it strange when Drago stood close to the buttons, blocking them from her view as he pressed a button to take them to their destination. Figuring he was doing it for safety reasons, she smiled. It was as if he didn't trust his 'future wife' with that information, like maybe he hadn't made his decision at all yet.

As they got off the elevator, it was Drago who led them this time. When he opened a door, she went in, but no one else followed her. Instead, they opened the next door.

"See ya later, Kat," Leo told her with a wink before going in.

"Later." *What?*

Chloe waived, actually, with a smile.

"Good luck, Kat." Maria gave a chuckle before closing the door.

Huh?

"I'll be back in a few minutes," Drago told her, wanting her to stay here.

She was confused, "Um, ok—"

Thud.

She stared at the door that was just shut in her face and started to get pissed. *Why does he do that!*

Walking into the apartment that sat next to his, he passed right by Maria and Chloe. "We need to talk," he ground out to Lucca, who was walking toward his woman, making him stop in his tracks.

Heading straight for the office in the boss's family apartment, Drago had a scratchy feeling under his skin the second that pink-haired girl had come into his presence today, and he had yet to shake it.

"Did you know she's a fucking math witch?!" he spat out the second Lucca shut the door to the office.

His underboss looked at him like he was crazy. "A math witch?"

"Yes, a math witch. She can fucking answer any math problem in a second without a damn calculator 'cause she *is* the fucking calculator!" Drago was pacing the room at this point, his voice turning more irate with each word passing his lips. "Did you know?"

"No, I didn't." Lucca seemed to be slightly impressed and amused but truthfully didn't appear to know. "It makes sense though."

"What does?" He stopped his pacing and looked him dead in the eyes.

"That she can do that."

He's fucking crazy. "How the fuck does that make sense?"

There was a hidden smile in his voice. "Look at Sal...."

I swear to fucking God. Drago slammed his eyes shut, becoming annoyed again. Sal was Lucifer's bastard child who became the great Salvatore; he was a fucking computer prodigy. "How in the hell did that fucking psychopath make them?"

Unlike him, the look that sat on Lucca's face showed that he wasn't the least bit surprised.

It all finally clicked with the chill that ran up his spine. Lucca was just as much a psychopath as Lucifer, and Lucca was a sick mastermind who had managed to orchestrate everything in his life just the way he wanted. They both might be crazy, but anything below a fucked-up genius they were not. He almost didn't want to ask.... "She's a fucking psychopath too, huh?"

The underboss sat back in his chair. This time his smile wasn't hidden. "Something tells me you'll be the one to find out if she is."

With my luck she will be. Running his hands through his hair, he was starting to get frustrated. "You fucker. I wanted the hot one. Why'd you have to go and bring her out from whatever fucking rock you found her under?"

"You still have time." Lucca leaned forward, his tone going dead serious. "Pick the fucking one they had almost played you into picking, for all I care. I thought you wanted revenge though, not their whore."

"I wanted both," he proclaimed, wishing it had been just that easy.

"No, you didn't." Lucca told him what he didn't know yet.

His words brought back his sense of reality, calming the itching that sat under his skin. He had wanted one thing and one thing only, and it was time he put that back in focus.

"She better not be crazy" was all he said as he headed out the door.

"Lucca! Guess what!" Leo said when he saw them come back into the main room. "Drago's girlfriend is a human calculator."

"So I've heard," Lucca sneered.

"She's not my fucking girlfriend," he mumbled under his breath, heading for the door to go back to where he'd left her.

Maria couldn't help herself. "Yeah, and he let her do the payroll."

Lucca's sneer fled. "He what?!"

"Yeah, and she thinks you're ugly." It was a low blow, and she hadn't exactly said that, but who gave a fuck.

Chloe gasped, grabbing Lucca's hand as if she couldn't believe it. She seemed to be more bothered by it than even he was.

"She said you're not her type," Maria proudly told him. "I guess there's no hope for you then, Drago."

Holding up his arm, he used his middle finger to flip off the whole Caruso family, who he was beginning to loath more and more each day. Some days, he didn't even know why he couldn't have stayed dead.

She turned around. A huge space greeted her. *Yep, this seems more like it.* This place was definitely a bachelor pad and definitely Drago's. It was cold, like a warehouse, with just the basics surrounding her. There was a leather couch with a glass coffee table, a dresser, and a big bed that sat catty-corner in the corner of the room, making it a studio apartment. The best part, however, was the kitchen and floor-to-ceiling windows on one side of the apartment that looked over Kansas City.

It was such a shame, really, because it could be such a great space, and it looked like it had been on its way there in the design phase since the kitchen seemed to be done, but the rest had just been dropped.

Taking another look at the space, she noticed the stairs that led up to a loft, making her wonder what was up there or if anything even was. But when her eyes landed on a wooden bat that was propped up against his bed, she was doubtful. *Probably not.*

The doorknob being turned had her spinning to look at the door. Unable to move an inch, she held her breath for the man she was loathing to finally be alone with. And it seemed like her luck might just have run out.

LIKE FATHER, LIKE DAUGHTER

T*he way he walked toward* her slowly should have scared her, but it didn't. She knew worse men than him, so there wasn't much he could do that hadn't already been done to her. . . besides being

Katarina headed over to gingerly pick up the glass of water, and when the liquid hit her lips, she couldn't help but knock the whole thing back, feeling a sudden dehydration. *Fuck, am I nervous?*

"Would you like something harder?" he asked, sensing her nerves.

"I'm eighteen, remember?"

Picking up her empty glass, he snatched it off the counter, mumbling under his breath, "Fuck, don't remind me."

Her brows furrowed together, hearing what seemed like disgust in his voice. She hadn't thought about him not liking their age difference, as she was the younger one. For her it wasn't the age difference that bothered Kat. She had to grow up fast, and even though her physical body might be eighteen, her soul and mind were much older. Too old. She didn't know how much older than her he was though. She figured late twenties, but maybe he was older than she had assumed. Licking her lips, she became curious. "How old are you?"

"Twenty-nine." Filling the glass once more, he sat it back down in front of her. He seemed to be just as curious. "Does that bother you?"

"It doesn't." Kat raised a brow. "But if it did, would it change anything?"

Staring at her with his dragon eyes, he answered honestly, with no remorse shining through, "No."

"I didn't think so," she whispered, sensing a hint of defeat that might be coming.

It was he who downed his drink this time.

If she had looked away, she might have missed it, but she could have sworn for a second that he felt sorry for her. However, it only lasted a second before it was gone. "Is this your place? Where we will live after...." Her voice trailed off. She wasn't able to say the words just yet.

"Yes." Again, he answered unapologetically. "Most of this floor is used as apartments for the Caruso soldiers."

Looking around the room once more, she noticed something. "You don't have a TV?"

"I'm not here that much to need one."

"Oh." She was reminded again that he mostly worked. She wondered if his bed was even that used, since he primarily stayed at the Caruso family home. "Do you mainly watch Leo, Maria, and Chloe?"

"If I'm not with them, I'm with the boss."

"I like them. They're really nice." She smiled, being truthful. They hadn't treated her like most people treated Lucianos, making her wonder.... She licked her lips nervously again. "Do they know... who I am?"

"If they didn't, do you think they would have treated you any differently?" he asked, turning the tables back on her.

"No." The word fell out her mouth. She knew they probably knew exactly who she was; they just didn't judge her for her last name. *Like he does.* Putting her eyes to the counter, she couldn't find herself to look at him for the next part. "I thought I would have scared *her*."

"I wasn't sure if you would either at first," he admitted, knowing exactly who she was talking about, before he paused, and his tone changed. "But you reminded Chloe of someone."

"Who?" Her eyes lifted back up to him.

He stared intently at her, wanting to see her reaction when the name passed his lips. "Sal."

Trying to keep herself together, she had to look back down at the counter. He was a brother she had never gotten to meet and only seen in pictures. Lucifer had left him to fend for himself on the street with his mother, and it had been shortly after her death when Dante, the Caruso boss, took him in as his own. Sal was a brother she might have never met but knew in her heart she related the most to. Their paths would have been much similar if it weren't for one person on this earth.

He took a step closer to the counter toward her. His height towered over hers. He wasn't going to push the topic of Sal, as it seemed to be a sensitive subject, but it was clear he wanted to know one thing. "How'd you know Chloe doesn't like to be touched?"

Katarina's black depths lifted to his once more. "How do you think?"

You could practically see the chill that crawled up his spine, though she was unsure if it was the words or the ominous sound in her voice that put it there. "But… you can be touched." He was stating the clear difference between her and Chloe. She didn't repel from touch, and she was able to take Leo's hand. Those were things the scarred girl could only do with Lucca.

"Because I had to learn to live with it." She sugarcoated it only slightly, only able to say the whole truth in her head. *With him.*

Confusion marked his face as he shook his head. "But you're his daughter."

Kat cleared her throat, knowing the only ones who would ever understand were the ones who had lived under that roof with Lucifer. Changing her tone to a lighter one, she had to force herself to let him believe that Chloe's scars ran deeper than hers. "Yeah, you're right."

His face didn't relax at first, still scrutinizing her with his gaze. It looked like he wanted to question her further, but instead something in him changed. He backed away and headed for a door off the kitchen. "I need to use the restroom. I'll be back."

Stunned at how quickly he left, she wasn't sure how she was doing anymore and if this plan Angel had was working. When he didn't come out right away, she made her way to the huge window. She looked down at the city and had never seen anything like it before. She'd never even dreamed places like this existed in Kansas City. It truly showed her how differently the Carusos and Lucianos lived. It was like they were from two different worlds.

"Is there a reason why you haven't finished your place?" she found herself asking when he reentered the room.

"What do you mean?"

Turning back, she looked at him. "Well, your kitchen looks finished, but not the rest."

"The kitchen's finished because it was in the contract with the contractor to have it finished." There seemed to be a sudden change that had overcome him within the few minutes he had left the room. Now, he was something darker. "And I haven't bothered to care about the rest because, like I said, I'm not here enough to give a fuck."

"Sorry I didn—"

Mumbling under his breath, he headed for the fridge again. "You're just going to be another kid I'll have to fucking babysit."

Did he just— "Excuse me?"

Stopping, Drago looked her dead in the eye. "You heard me."

She took a step away from the window, toward him. "If you were worried about babysitting another *kid,* then why did you pick me?"

He was the one to take a step toward her this time. The sinister tone that coated his voice enunciated each word, showing no remorse. "You. Know. Why."

Katarina felt a shift begin in her. *Stay calm, remember what Angel said.* She had known why he'd picked her all along; this just confirmed it. Taking a deep breath, she started walking away hoping somehow, she just could, but a different voice entered her head....

Give him hell.

A smile graced her lips before she picked up the wooden bat that was propped up against his bed.

"What are yo—"

She gripped the neck of the bat. The skin around her black fingernail polish turned whiter before she crashed it down on the glass table.

"ARE YOU FUCKING CRAZY?" Drago boomed, looking at the shattered glass that sprinkled all over the room.

When she started heading toward him with a glow in her black eyes, he moved the fuck out of the way right before she swung the bat, clearing off one of his kitchen counters. By the time he made it to the other side of the room, Lucca rushed into the room and was followed by Maria and Leo.

"What the fuck is going on here?" Lucca asked before his eyes went wide when he saw Kat with the bat in her hands.

"Whoa! Cool." Leo seemed to be more impressed with this side of her.

Maria just took in the sight.

"I knew she had to be fucking crazy. Like father, like daughter!" Drago hissed loudly over the noise, so she could hear it.

"In that case…," Kat yelled before rearing the bat back and swinging as hard as she could at the pots and pans that were hanging above his island, sending most of the pans flying and crashing down.

"I'm gonna kill that little bit—"

Lucca grabbed his shoulder, keeping him in his place.

Throwing the bat on her shoulder, she walked over to stand right in front of the big bastard.

"You done?" Drago asked her, becoming irate.

"Yep." She threw the bat down, flipping it over her shoulder as she started to walk out. "Lemme know if you would like to babysit me again, asshole."

Everyone behind her blinked for several moments as they looked around at the destruction she created in just minutes.

Maria, however, turned to Drago. "I'll marry her if you don't."

LUCIFER'S WORLD

Before the elevator door could close, a hand on the other side stopped it, making the doors slide open to reveal Lucca.

Kat swallowed hard.

Stepping onto the elevator, he gave her his back. "I'll be taking you home now."

Well, shit.

"You two would be fucking perfect for each other," Drago spat, picking up the pots and pans, and if they could have procreated to mix their blood, he'd fucking let her have the witch.

An unbothered Maria smiled at him.

"Kat really did all this?" Chloe asked, holding the broom.

"Yeah, it was awesome." Leo laughed, helping him pick up.

Drago was on the verge of sending the Caruso children flying out the window.

"Why would she do it?" Chloe asked, not understanding what could have changed her into The Hulk.

Maria, who had brushed off all the glass from the couch, lazily sat down and started talking as if she'd been here the whole time. "He made her do it."

"I did not," Drago hissed at the prissy blonde. "Now, how about you actually help and stop fucking bugging me?"

"I'm wearing my good heels," she told him before revealing the red bottom. The shift in her voice should have warned him what was about to come. "I just wanna know one thing...."

Rolling his eyes, he angrily looked at her. "What?"

"Did you piss her off to make *her* hate *you*—" His stomach began to sink with the words that left her mouth next. "Or did you piss her off to make *you* hate *her*?"

Sitting next to the boogieman in the Cadillac sent chills up her spine. When she told them earlier that Lucca wasn't her type, she'd really meant that he scared the fuck out of her. There was no way you could be raised by her father and not see it. To see when a man was truly mad and needed to be buried behind bars or six feet in the dirt. She could see every drop of blood he had washed away, every emotion he would never feel, and everything he was made of.

The second his blue-green eyes landed on her for the first time, it was like the air in the room had suddenly become thicker, and she knew she was in the presence of a man who could do terrible, horrendous things to any living being in the blink of an eye.

Lucca had been the one to finally take down her father because only men like that were gifted to take out men of their own kind. It was sick, really. You needed one monster to bring down another, but who was going to take down that monster when he finally became the man they had to destroy?

"What you did isn't going to change his mind," he told her, breaking the deafening silence.

"I know," Kat whispered.

"Then why do it?"

She didn't hold back the truth. "Because he's an asshole."

"There're worse men out there, Katarina." He said it as if it was a warning.

"I'm sure there are, but that doesn't make me want to marry him."

Lucca was silent for several moments while he gripped the leather steering wheel of the Cadillac. "Do you know why out of all my men I picked him to fulfil the marriage agreement?"

All she could manage was to shake her head. Unsure if she wanted to hear what he had to say next.

"I know no one else more dedicated, resilient, and loyal than Drago. He has never disappointed me, and I wouldn't trade him for a hundred men." He looked as though he was picking his words carefully, wanting her to fully understand. "He has the making of being a great husband, and I fully believe that one day he will. You just have to give him a chance."

It was her this time who went silent. Knowing who and what Lucca was, she was sure he wasn't wrong. She could live with marrying Drago to save her family and had practically accepted it the moment he'd chosen her, but one thought scared her. Finally, she decided to reveal the truth on a whisper. "I can't leave Cassius."

Lucca's eyes drifted over to her before they had to return to the road. His tone changed, becoming even more serious than he already was. "Why?"

Looking down at her feet on the floorboard, she told him all she could, "He just needs me."

Nodding in understanding, he acknowledged her but didn't give her any false promises.

Thankful when he pulled into her driveway and parked, she almost couldn't get out of the car fast enough, but the boogieman didn't let her go that easily.

He dropped his voice an octave and gave her his final words. "Don't prove him right by being exactly how he thought you'd be, Katarina."

Swallowing what had risen in her throat, she got out of the car and slammed the door shut, knowing she had done just that. Proved the Luciano blood was tainted, *and that we're nothing but trash.*

Dominic came out on the front porch. "What'd you do?" he asked, seeing Lucca had gotten out of the car to lean up against it to smoke a cigarette, knowing it must have been bad for him to drop her off.

"I gave him hell," she told him as she stomped onto the porch.

Dominic stared at her for a second before he proudly smiled, raising his hand as she passed for a high five. "That's my girl."

Pushing the curtain out of the way when she entered the house, she looked out the window and watched her brother talk with Lucca.

"Why is he here?" Matthias asked after coming over to see what she was looking at.

"I may or may not have done something bad."

Matthias got a nervous look in his eyes.

"What'd you do?" Cassius asked, coming up behind her.

"I took a baseball bat to Drago's apartment."

"Badass." Her little brother took a glance at the two outside before he walked away.

Her other brother, however, looked like he was going to be sick.

Kat knew it was because Angel was still in their grasp. "It's going to be all right." Now, her stomach turned. Seeing him like this made her feel remorse. "Dominic always makes everything better." At least she hoped and prayed. For his sake, not hers.

"Did you see him?" he solemnly asked.

Her mouth ran dry, wishing he had forgotten to ask while she nodded her head.

The lightness in his eyes finally returned. "How is he?"

Never in a million years could she have the heart to tell him the truth. To tell him that while he sat here dying a little more every day, the one who was captured was surviving just fine without him. "He's okay."

And just like that, the light evaporated from his eyes.

Grabbing his hand, she gave it a squeeze, knowing he needed to hear something, anything to feel closer to his twin. Kat needed to reassure him his brother was still just that, his brother. Even if it meant she had to lie. "He misses you."

That was all he needed to return the light and give him hope. She wondered what would happen to Matthias... when he realized all hope was gone.

Drago was still heated when he was called into Lucca's office, and he knew fucking exactly what he wanted to talk about. *About that little psycho math witch.*

"The deal will not work if you mistreat her," Lucca told him with a puff of smoke escaping from his lips.

Was he hearing him fucking right? "Me, mistreat her?!"

"Yes." His underboss was harsh, knowing exactly what he had done.

The truth was, it was hard for him to admit it. He didn't have a damn reason not to like that cute pink-haired smartass, except for the last name she carried, and that scared the fuck out of him. As bad as it sounded, the only way this worked for him was if he hated her.

He had excused himself to the bathroom because he felt something different under the itching of his skin. Making him take a hard look at himself in the mirror, knowing when he came out, he needed to be who he truly was to her, a fucking asshole. Or that itch just might never go away.

Lucca could probably see the turmoil going on in his head. "What do you want to do, Drago?"

It was tempting to tell him to hell with Katarina and choose someone, anyone else from the Luciano family, but the man inside of him they had killed knew there was only one choice to satiate his need for revenge. At least that was what he was going to choose to believe… for now.

"You can choose someone e—"

"No." Drago stopped his underboss right there with a boom from his chest. There was going to be no going back anymore, or what ifs. This was it. "Katarina is mine."

Kat sat up in bed when the light entered her room and her oldest brother came in. When she saw the worried lines on his face by the glowing light, her heart sank for him.

Taking a seat on the edge of her bed, he gave her his back, unable to look at her. She was unsure of how many minutes had passed when he finally spoke into the darkness. "Did I ever tell you about when I first saw you?"

She pulled her knees to her chest, not recalling if he had or not. "I don't think so."

"You were the fucking cutest, chubbiest baby. I thought there was no way you were my sister because I couldn't believe *he* created you."

Kat smiled, beginning to listen…

…Almost every night was the same for the eleven-year-old. Every night, he would sit down with his father at the kitchen table, and while Lucifer counted his money, Dominic cleaned the guns knowing each one almost inside and out. However, this night was different.

The banging on the door started when the final gun had been racked, and when his father didn't make a move, Dominic got up to answer it. He almost missed it at first, seeing no one standing on the other side of the door, but then he saw something squirm at the bottom of his feet, and finally, he knew what lay on the porch. "Dad…."

"What is it?" Lucifer asked, getting up from the kitchen table. He only looked at the thing for a second before he headed back to his seat. "Get rid of it."

Looking down at the snuggled-up contents, he picked up the pink blanket that was wrapped around a beautiful baby girl. The blond hair on her head had him wondering why in all the houses in Kansas City they had picked this one, but when his eyes met her black ones, there was no denying it. Taking her in the warm house, he glanced at his father. "Is she yo—"

"Don't know, don't care."

Dominic had to think for a minute…. "I think there's some baby stuff still in the basement."

"I said to get fucking rid of it," Lucifer demanded with his hot tongue.

"But it's dark and cold outside."

The devilish man abruptly stood, going for the baby. "Fine, I will."

"No." The young boy did his best to match his father's tone. "Let her stay for the night, then I can in the morning."

His father stared at him with that crazed look in his eye before he threatened him, "I better not see or hear that thing, do you understand?"

Nodding his head, he quickly walked to the basement door to get her out of sight before the devil changed his mind.

The six-year-old twin brothers followed closely behind, wanting to follow their brother instead of being alone with their father.

"What is it?" Angel asked when they reached the bottom of the steps into the cold basement.

"Hold out your arms, strong arms, strong arms," he coached him as he placed the chunky baby in his little arms. "It's your baby sister."

Matthias looked at the pink bundle in his twin's arms. "Our sister?"

"Yes." Dominic began pulling a wooden cage into the middle of the room, then dusting it off as best as he could before going back to his brothers. He bent over, meeting them eye to eye, getting their full attention. "And we have to protect her. Can you help me with that?"

Angel was the first to bravely nod his head, then Matthias followed.

Picking her up and placing her in the old crib all the Luciano brothers had used, Dominic figured she was about a year old or so by remembering how the twins had looked when they were younger.

He'd been trying to keep his brothers alive since he was five years old, and he hoped he could do it again, but something told him this time was going to be different considering this one was a girl. Lucifer wanted an army, grooming his boys since birth into men who would one day control the city. The only women in his life were the many he used to try and fulfill those dreams, throwing them away when they never got pregnant or if it wasn't a boy in her belly.

There was no place in Lucifer's world for a girl. Let alone a baby girl.

Angel looked up at him with almost the same dark eyes she carried. "What's her name?"

Reaching down when she twisted the blanket open, he touched the chubby baby's onesie that was light pink and covered in cute little cats. He heard a name before somewhere, unsure if it was on TV or in a book, but he had liked it, thinking from time to time of the beautiful name when he had been reminded of it.

"Katarina."...

...There was no one on this earth she loved more than her oldest brother, Dominic. He had always been and still was her savior, but in her heart, she knew then he could no longer save her.

It was a beautiful story, but that wasn't why he had come in here.... "He still wants me, doesn't he?"

"I'm so sorry, Kat." Dominic's head fell in his hands. "I'm so fucking sorry."

THE PRINCESS IS OUT OF HER CASTLE

"This sucks." *She slammed down* a pile of her clothes in a box. She had been packing all her shit up for the last day. Basically, just her personal items she couldn't live without, her makeup, and her clothes. She would leave some of her stuff here for when she visited. "Wait, I won't be like Angel, will I?"

"Who are you talking to?" Cassius asked coming into her room.

"Just my Shadow."

"All right." Her youngest brother looked at her like she was crazy. "There's some hot girl for you."

What did he just say? "Huh?"

"Some hot girl showed up at our door to see you. I think she's a Caruso 'cause she showed up with a suit. Better hurry though. Matthias won't stop staring at her, and it seems like Dominic hates her."

"Oh God." Kat dropped whatever was in her hands knowing exactly who it was. Flying out her door, she went into the living room to see the tall-legged blonde. "Maria?"

FIVE MINUTES EARLIER

Knocking on the Luciano front door gave her pleasure. She loved ruining someone's day.

When the door flew open, she was greeted with Angel's other half. They might have looked like the same person, but they couldn't have been more opposite. Whereas she was beginning to like Angel, this one, however....

"Hey, princess." The head-to-toe inked brother smiled as his eyes traveled down her body.

I did not. That mask he put on the second he opened the door and saw it was her, she couldn't miss. Matthias put on a façade fooling those around him, but he didn't fool her for a second. She could see right through that mask for what he was... *broken.*

Todd, her bodyguard, barreled through the door pushing the twin out of the way to check the house before she went in.

"Who the fuck are you?" Dominic stood when he entered.

Maria steeped into the house before Todd got killed. "He's with me."

This time, it was Dominic whose eyes went down the length of her tall body, taking in her high heels, short dress, and fur coat.

"Why the hell are you here?"

It'd had been a long time since she had seen the oldest Luciano brother. At the time, she hadn't been a woman, so she hadn't taken a good look at him. Now, as she took in his appearance, he looked much different than the twins and Kat. Whereas they were pale with gray eyes that were almost black, Dominic had tanned skin that matched his chocolate hair and set off the brown in his hazel eyes, but it was the beautiful green in them that made them sparkle.

"I, um—" She had to think a minute what it was exactly she came for. "To see Kat."

"And what do you want with her?" He crossed his strong arms over his chest.

"Well, I thought she needed a wedding dress." Maria raised a perfectly manicured brow. "Doesn't she?"

"Cassius."

She turned her head when a young boy stood up from the couch. He looked as if he was Dominic's Mini-Me. Both brothers baring no resemblance to their father.

"Go get Kat," Dominic ordered without looking away from the blonde.

Staring at the little Luciano for a moment longer, she tilted her head to the side, seeing something different in the boy that was… almost reminiscent… but then he walked away.

"Can I take your coat?" Matthias asked, clearly wanting to see her without the long thing as he reached to help her out of it.

"Touch me, and I'll kill you," she threatened with the sweetest smile.

Matthias didn't take a step closer, somehow knowing that smile was an act.

The oldest brother, however, took a step toward her, unafraid of her or the bodyguard she'd come with. "Does Lucca know the princess is out of her castle?"

That smile didn't disappear from her face. "Do you think I would be here if he did?"

"Certainly not." He looked at the suit that came with her. "If this is the one who brought you."

It took a minute before Todd realized he'd been insulted.

His hazel eyes moved back to her. "I hope the poor sucker knows whatever you promised him won't be worth it by the time Lucca gets done with him."

"What he doesn't know won't hurt him." Placing a tall heel in front of the other, she made the distance between them that much smaller. "It can be our little secret."

Most men on this earth weren't worth a second glance, but this time, she finally let her eyes glance down his body. For some reason he was different than she expected. She thought he'd be weak since agreeing to all the Caruso terms, but now she could see that might not be the case at all…

Out of all the Luciano brothers, this one, she liked. A lot.

"What are you doing here?" Kat asked when the Caruso girl didn't stop the stare-off she was having with her oldest brother.

Finally, after another moment, she broke their eye contact. "I thought you might want a wedding dress for when you walk down the aisle."

"I have a white dress, but it's shor—"

"Absolutely not." Maria stopped her right there before she could finish the word. She looked flat-out offended. "I am taking you shopping right now."

"O-Okay," Katarina agreed, afraid if she didn't, the girl might cut her head off. She couldn't have cared less if she walked down in what she was wearing right now, but she damn sure wasn't about to tell her that.

"I'm going with you," Dominic announced, grabbing his coat. "Matthias, you stay here with Cassius."

Matthias, who was grabbing his jacket too, looked defeated.

"That won't be necces—"

Dominic raised his hand, cutting her off. "I'm not having Lucca find out I let you two go alone with this fucking idiot."

Again, it took Todd forever to figure out he was talking about him. "Excuse m—"

"Fine," Maria agreed.

She picked up her fur-lined leather jacket, and they all headed out the door, leaving Cassius and a heartbroken Matthias behind.

When he saw the Cadillac they'd showed up in, Dom stopped in his tracks. "You know what, Ted—"

"Todd," Maria corrected.

"Todd," he repeated the correct name, getting the Caruso's guard's attention. "How about you go home, and we can all just pretend Maria snuck out by herself. I think we both know I won't touch a pretty blond hair on her head because of what Lucca would do to me if he found out I did. I'm sure it's going to be similar to what he's going to fucking do to you if you don't leave."

Her bodyguard's face went pale as she waved him to go, and he left running. "Bye, Todd."

Well, he'll be dead soon.

As she walked toward her brother's car, the cold February air hit her face on a gust of wind. She looked at what the blonde was wearing. "Aren't you cold?"

It was Dominic who answered her. "You can't feel cold if your heart is dead." Giving a deadly smile to the golden goddess, he opened the passenger door of his blacked-out Mustang for her. "Isn't that right, princess?"

Did he just.... She was going to have one of her talks with Cassius tonight about how boys can show their feelings to girls in many different ways.

Dominic didn't hate her... He fucking liked her.

THE RIGHT ONE

"U*m, where are we going?"* she asked when Maria started walking into the expensive department store side of the mall. The side she never visited because it was ridiculously priced and outrageously stupid.

"I told you, finding a wedding dress."

She began looking around at the nudes and golds everywhere on display and how spaced out everything was from another ridiculously priced item before she planted her feet firmly on the ground. "Not from here, we're not."

"Yes, we are," she stated, clearly daring Kat to no longer challenge her about it while she grabbed her arm to get her to move. "A girl only gets to walk down the aisle for the first time once. So, it has to be designer."

"Princess has a point." This time, Dominic grabbed her other arm, pulling her along.

"Fine." She reluctantly let them drag her along thinking if Dom had said it was ok— *Wait.* "Did you just say, *for the first time once*?"

Still pulling her along, she didn't even hesitate to speak. "I'm thinking my third husband after the first two mysteriously died will be the right one."

"That's good to know," Dominic muttered under his breath.

"Maria…."

The blonde looked over at her.

"I think I'm a little bit scared of you."

"I'm only kidding." She smiled with a hint of evil, showing she probably wasn't joking.

The truth was, if she were a man, she would be very fucking afraid of her, but Maria gave off a female empowerment vibe. It was obvious to her and her brothers that the mafia princess was a straight-up psychopath like her brother Lucca, but there was a difference between them... She had been born a woman. And like Kat knew all too well, they would *never* be treated like their brothers. No matter how strong or smart they could become, in their father's eyes and in the mafia world, they would never be as strong or as smart as their sons.

Because of that, there seemed to be a woman code written into Maria's DNA, and she was pretty sure the blonde wouldn't hurt a woman for a million dollars. Therefore, she liked Maria, even if it was a little sexist that she liked her and not Lucca.

When they reached a bunch of little stores off to the sides of the mall that had the big designer names above them, they headed into one that consisted of nothing but white dresses.

A very beautiful man with killer bone structure greeted them before heading to Maria and giving her kisses on each cheek. "Maria, my love, I haven't seen you in a while."

"I know. I've missed you." She grabbed his hand begging to introduce him to her entourage. "Ken, I need a dress for my friend Kat."

Ken? Yep, that was exactly whom he looked like, straight from the Barbie dream house in his tux.

Ken looked at Dominic, eyeing him up and down like he was his next meal. "And who might this handsome man be?"

"This is her brother Dominic." Maria smiled, probably a bit to happily, at what was happening.

"Nice to meet you, Dominic." Ken winked before quickly looking at Kat. "And you are gorgeous. Spin for me, honey, let me take a look at you."

Slowly, she spun for him, feeling a bit awkward as she did so.

"Maria, you take her to the dressing room to get her undressed while I go pull some dresses." His eyes moved back to Dom. "And you, handsome, can go take a seat in the sitting area."

"Thanks." Dominic politely smiled at him as they went to do as ordered.

When they entered the dressing room area in the back, there was a huge, lavish velvet couch for them to sit on while she tried on the dresses.

"May I offer you some champagne?" a woman in a tight black dress offered, carrying in three glasses of it.

Dominic quickly took a glass, downing the contents in a second, clearly looking like he needed it before he graciously handed a glass to Maria and then taking the last one for himself. Clearly afraid of looking greedy, he started to explain himself. "She's not old enough to drink."

The woman looked a bit mortified, taking another glance at Kat since she was the one needing a dress.

"But not too young to get married," he told her.

Gotta love America.

"Okay, now you go in here." Maria opened the door to the dressing room with her champagne in hand. "And put that robe on, and Ken will be in here in a minute."

"And how exactly do you know that... and Ken?" she asked, feeling like she was probably asking a dumb fucking question.

"Because I used to come in here all the time to try on dresses for fun," Maria answered just as stupidly as she had thought.

"Right... okay." Going into the dressing room, she quickly undressed out of her black clothes, placing them in the chair and throwing on the white robe like she was told.

God, what am I doing?!

She wasn't in there long enough to regret her decision before Ken entered with a handful of dresses and had her in one in just a few minutes.

When she came back out of the dressing room, Maria's eyes lit up as she stepped up onto a pedestal.

As she took that first look at herself in the mirror, Katarina felt… strange. The expensive white dress was stunning, but it didn't feel like her. "Hmm."

The light in Maria's eyes dimmed when she didn't seem to like it and became more critical of it herself.

Dominic gave it a hard stare, then shook his head. "I don't like it."

They went back into the dressing room to put on another gown and doing the whole thing over again only to come out to feel even less like herself when she looked at her reflection.

"No," Dominic stated, taking another sip of champagne.

Ken's mouth dropped open in apparent offense at how no one was taking a second look at the couture dresses he had pulled.

Not wanting to waste Ken's time any longer, she wanted the fake fairytale to end. "The dress I have is fine, Maria."

Seeing her distress, Maria stood, coming closer to her to talk. "What's wrong?"

"They're beautiful, but—" She halted, then looked back at herself in the mirror. "This just… isn't me."

"Go back in there and get this thing off," Maria ordered her after it looked like a lightbulb had gone off in her head. "I'll be right back."

They went back into the room, where Ken helped her out of the dress, and when Maria entered, this time with a much different dress both Kat's and Ken's jaws dropped.

When she put the dress on and came out of the room, she didn't even have to look in the mirror to know it was the one.

"It's perfect," the blonde whispered in awe.

Now, as she looked at her brother, Kat would have sworn she saw his eyes turn a bit glossy for just a moment right before he blinked it away. He was only able to manage one word. "Wow."

A MISSION TO GET EVERY MAN IN KANSAS CITY

K*at couldn't have heard the* price correctly as they stood at the register with the dress. "Excuse me, what?"

Maria dipped into her purse. "Don't worry about it. It's a gift from—"

"The Carusos," a dark voice spoke behind them before he slid a black card onto the desk.

Oh no. "I really can't accept—"

"It's okay, Kat." Dominic pulled her closer to him by throwing an arm over her shoulder. "It's the least they could do."

The next few minutes were unbearably awkward while the dress was being paid for and she was told to return in a week to pick it up after the alterations were finished.

It wasn't until they left the bridal store that Lucca finally spoke his mind, and when he did, he didn't raise his voice, instead speaking quietly, making it all the more frightening. "Maria, you have five seconds to tell me why you are here."

She just flipped her hair, simply saying, "Kat needed a dress."

"And where the fuck are my men?"

When she didn't answer right away, it was Dom who spoke, "Kat asked me to drop her off here, and when I came, I saw Maria alone." He lied trying to save the dumbass Caruso. This next part, however, wasn't a lie, and he looked Lucca right in the eye to prove it. "Instead of getting her in trouble, I decided to watch her for you and was going to bring her back home safely when they were done."

Maria nodded, adding to the lie when Lucca looked like he was about to kill Dominic. "I called Kat to meet me here, and then I just snuck out and took a cab here."

After another second of staring her brother down, he changed his attention to Maria. Now it looked like he just wanted to kill her. "We're leaving."

"Yep, so are we." Dominic pulled Kat with him, who was still under his arm at the opposite side of the Caruso siblings.

"Bye, Kat." An unbothered Maria waved.

Looking back, she smirked at the brave girl. "Bye, thank you for everything."

"You're welcome." Maria's smiling eyes moved to the Luciano brother before he got too far. "Bye, Dominic."

He, on the other hand, just kept walking, giving her his back, pretending he hadn't heard her.

It wasn't until then that Maria appeared to be very… bothered.

"That was rude," she whispered to her brother.

"Don't care." Dominic slowed down a bit when they got farther from the Caruso siblings. "That psycho is on a mission to get every man in Kansas City murdered today, and I'm sure as fuck not going to be one of them."

RSVP

You are cordially invited to the wedding of

Katarina Luciano

to

Drago De Santis

Saturday, the Twenty-Eighth of February
at seven o'clock in the evening.

St. Rose Catholic Church

RSVP

WE KNEW THIS DAY WOULD COME

It was going to be a day no one thought would come.

The day when a Caruso would marry a Luciano.

The event of a lifetime.

And it was finally here.

"May I come in?"

Kat's sorrow-filled eyes went to the door and saw Angel standing there. She managed a nod, and he came in, carefully sitting down beside her.

They were quietly watching the clock move closer and closer to seven. The air in the room felt almost as heavy as the weight on their shoulders.

Licking her dry lips, she tried to speak. "When I do this… there's no going back for us, is there?"

His eyes didn't move from the clock. "No, there isn't."

A shaky breath came out when her fears were confirmed. This marriage wasn't just sealing her fate. It was sealing Angel's too.

"As long as you're a Caruso, I will be too."

The tear that had been captured in her eye finally slipped free at his words. Regardless of what happened with Angel and the Caruso girl he loved, he could have finally walked free when Lucca let him go. Her marrying Drago, however, was going to take that away from him forever. He wasn't going to leave her here in the hands of the Carusos without a Luciano on the inside to protect her. Him gaining Lucca's trust more and more every day as well as being in love with a Caruso made him that inside man.

But as sad as she felt for Angel, there was someone her heart hurt just a little bit more for. "I don't know how much longer he has...."

"You let me worry about Matthias." Her brother grabbed her hand. "You just get married and save all our asses."

Reminded of why she was about to do this, she wiped the tear and held in the rest that were threatening to ruin her makeup.

Giving her hand a final squeeze, he stood tall as he looked down on his little sister while she sat there in her beautiful wedding dress. "They can make us dress differently, act differently, and even change your last name, Katarina, but they *can't* change where we were born, who our father is, or *our blood*." There was a sudden sadness that veiled him. "Not even we can."

Drago was looking into the mirror finishing tightening up his black tie when a different reflection appeared behind him. Turning, he looked at a very different-looking Dominic, man to man. This wasn't the Luciano brother he had seen with his underboss; this was a man coming to protect what was his.

"You do anything to hurt her or be any fucking less than what Lucca has said about you,"—Dominic began making him promise—"you'll have wished the boogieman had come for you when I fucking kill you." Unafraid of who stood before him, he gave him a glimpse of who Dominic truly was.... "And this time, there will be no coming back, Drago, because unlike my father, I don't fucking miss."

That was the first time he really met Dominic Luciano, and his first taste of revenge.

"You ready?"

Seeing Dominic come into her waiting room, she stood and took a few deep breaths.

His fierce hazel eyes stared at her black ones. "I want you to know that even if it meant my death, I would not let you walk down this aisle if I didn't know you could handle it."

"I know," she whispered strongly.

"We knew this day would come, Katarina."...

...They had sat in Dominic's Mustang eating doughnuts with the words "Happy Birthday" on them in pink frosting. Normal people celebrated their birthdays on the day they were born, but being one of the unlucky ones, she didn't. She celebrated her birthday on the day she'd apparently showed up on the doorstep. It had been seventeen years since that day, and she was definitely eighteen by now.

There was no record of whoever she had been before she was placed on that porch. Only one thing was for sure, that Lucifer was her biological father. Dominic had made Katarina Luciano exist, and that was more than anyone else had done for her. She supposed it would bother someone to not know where they had come from, but the truth was, her mother was probably dead in a ditch somewhere, knowing her father, and to get him to tell her who she was wasn't happening, and that was if he even knew. However, she had her brothers, and that was more than enough family for her.

Putting a half-eaten doughnut back in the box, Dominic looked over at her, his face etched into a serious expression. "Things are about to change, Kat. I feel it."

She slowly swallowed the bite she had in her mouth, knowing their father was becoming more uncontrollable and irate by the day. "I feel it too."

"There's going to be a day when I won't be able to protect you any longer, Katarina. You're eighteen now, and I'm afraid there will be nothing I can do." She could see his heavy heart getting heavier. "But you'll be ready. It's what we've been preparing for."

Nodding her head, she knew his words to be true. It was almost like a timer had been started, and no matter how ready she would be, Kat just hoped the clock would never run out...

…"Yes, we did." She smiled at the memory.

"You're going to be the one to save us all, and I couldn't be more fucking proud." Dominic's intense gaze still bore into hers while his voice matched the intensity. "They might not know what you're capable of, but one day they will. They'll know what we are all capable of."

There wasn't another man on this earth like him, who had been through what he had been through, had seen what he had seen. She was convinced there was no man stronger than Dominic. He was the Lucianos' future, and he was going to even the score.

Smiling down at her, he had one final request that he had made once before. "Make him fuckin' regret picking you, Kat…. Give. Him. Hell."

"I plan on it." She smiled back.

Kat had been the one to be saved by her brothers for years, but this time it was her turn to save them. Her turn to save the family and finally prove her father wrong.

There was a place in this family for women, and like her brother had said, *I couldn't be more fucking proud.*

Putting her hand through Dominic's arm, she picked up the small bouquet of dark red roses.

The clock had finally struck seven.

UNTIL DEATH DO US PART

O*nce the doors flung open,* the Catholic church not only echoed with the organs that began to play but with the gasps. Both the Luciano and Caruso sides were shocked upon seeing the first glimpse of the bride. Even the priest was taken aback.

As she walked down the aisle, her heavy dress dragged behind her while her lacy veil trailed a foot behind. It was exactly how you pictured a Catholic wedding dress to be in all its grand glory, all except for one thing.... Her dress was as black as her eyes, and her veil was as dark as her past.

This was a statement, an almost protest. There wasn't only a wedding about to take place, but a funeral. It was a final goodbye to the life she was leaving behind and to her last name.

Lastly, this dress was her. It made her pale skin glisten and her light pink tresses glow underneath the lace. Her dark eyeshadow only added to the effect, making her look like a regal gothic queen.

When they reached the end of the aisle, Dominic was forced to give his sister away with a final hug. Even though they were prepared, that moment was harder on both of them than they'd thought it would be. You could see when he looked down at her that he still pictured her as the baby who had shown up on the doorstep in the cat onesie, and she still pictured him as the big brother who would always be there to protect her. However, they were both no longer those things, and it was time to part.

Giving her to the man who had stood at the end of the aisle, he left and took a seat.

When her eyes landed on Drago for the first time since she had trashed his place, she expected the man who held a bit of fury behind his eyes. Especially with her dress choice, she had expected to see the flames in his fiery eyes. That wasn't what she got though. There was a real calm in them, and as he looked down upon her for the first time since she'd approached the altar, he seemed almost pleased.

Unlike the Carusos, religion wasn't anything her family practiced, but being married in their faith was what made them happy. It made her wonder what they had told or done to the priest to get him to marry them. All Kat knew was that Catholic weddings were one hell of a long event, and everything seemed to blur until she heard the words….

"Dearly beloved, you have come together into the house of the Church, so that in the presence of the Church's minister and community, your intention to enter into Marriage may be strengthened by the Lord with a sacred seal. Christ abundantly blesses the love that binds you. Through a special Sacrament, he enriches and strengthens those he has already consecrated by Holy Baptism, that they may be faithful to each other forever and assume all the responsibilities of married life. And so, in the presence of the Church, I ask you to state your intentions.

"Drago and Katarina, have you come here to enter into Marriage without coercion, freely and wholeheartedly?"

Together they said the words, "I have."

"Are you prepared, as you follow the path of Marriage, to love and honor each other for as long as you both shall live?"

"I am," they repeated together again.

"Are you prepared to accept children lovingly from God and to bring them up according to the law of Christ and his Church?"

Drago repeated, "I am," for the final time, but Kat took a moment to think about those particular words from the priest before she finally had to say the words, "I am."

"Since it is your intention to enter into the covenant of Holy Matrimony, join your right hands, and declare your consent before God and his Church."

Her heart started to pound out of her chest as she gently raised her right hand, and everything seemed to go in slow motion.

Taking her small hand in his, he gave her his vows, "I, Drago, take you, Katarina, for my lawful wife, to have and to hold, from this day forward, for better, for worse, for richer, for poorer, in sickness and in health, until death do us part."

She had been told to memorize the vows, because without the priest's coaching, it gave them more meaning. Drago had done it so easily, and she found it more difficult, only able to hear the pounding of her heart as they waited patiently for her vows. It wasn't until his thumb lightly brushed over her knuckles that she found herself saying, "I, Katarina, take you, Drago,"— she stared down at the way he tenderly held her hand and was able to continue—"for my lawful husband, to have and to hold, from this day forward, for better, for worse, for richer, for poorer, in sickness and in health,"—her eyes finally trailed back up to his, and she was able to see that in this moment they were in this together. That, just like her, it wasn't what he might have wanted, but it was something he had to do. Unfortunately for her, she was who he chose, becoming collateral damage in this deadly game of chess. Slowly, her heart ceased, and there was nothing but her voice left—"until death do us part."

The priest laid his frail hand over theirs, sacramentally making the bride and groom become wife and husband with no turning back. "May the Lord in his kindness strengthen the consent you have declared before the Church,

and graciously bring to fulfillment his blessing within you. What God joins together, let no one put asunder."

"Amen." The church echoed with the voices in the room.

Picking up the rings, he began blessing the tiny pieces of metal. "May the Lord bless these rings, which you give to each other as a sign of love and fidelity."

Drago picked up the blessed ring and slid it onto her finger.

"Katarina, receive this ring as a sign of my love and fidelity. In the name of the Father, and of the Son, and of the Holy Spirit."

She looked down. A dainty platinum wedding ring now sat on her left ring finger, and whether she liked it or not, she was a wife. Kat picked up the weighted thick band that looked like silver that had been brushed in black. "Drago, receive this ring as a sign of my love and fidelity. In the name of the Father, and of the Son, and of the Holy Spirit."

She slid the ring on what she'd never thought she'd say in a million years... *my husband.*

A TWENTY-FIRST-CENTURY ARRANGED MARRIAGE...

T*here was no ceremonial kiss* in a Catholic wedding, *thank God*, as it would have been one hell of an awkward first kiss. That was what she had been the most grateful for out of this whole day.

The reception was being held in the ballroom at the casino hotel, and only the bravest of the Lucianos had come to be put in a box with the Carusos on their home ground.

You could tell that everyone in the room was on edge as they all sat at their tables eating the full-course meals that had been prepared. Some of the Luciano men even refused to eat, afraid of being poisoned.

Looking around the huge ballroom, she had to give Maria credit, knowing it was all her doing. Everything about the wedding had been breathtaking. The room was a full black and white tie affair, and the only pops of color were the splashes of red roses throughout the room.

"It's time for the first dance," Maria told them as she came over after everyone finished their dessert.

Kat quickly looked over at Drago, who didn't seem interested in it either. "That's okay. I don't—"

"I would like to welcome up our bride and groom to the dance floor for their first dance," the lead singer of the wedding band spoke into the microphone.

The room went silent at first, but when Dante, the Caruso boss, began clapping his hands, everyone else followed.

Drago pushed back his chair and stood, asking for her hand by holding out his.

Taking it, she let him lead her to the open dance floor, and the band began playing while the singer opened his mouth to sing the song *What Would It Take.*

When his hand reached behind to the small of her back, the two started swaying to the music, and she quickly became shocked since he had the body type of a football player. "You know how to dance?"

"I know how to slow dance without stepping on your toes, yes."

Kat actually smiled up at him as the words 'love me' were sung. Hearing that, she quickly looked away, swearing to herself she was going to kill Maria for the song choice.

Her eyes drifted out to the crowd while they danced, looking for one person in particular.

"I haven't seen him," Drago whispered to her.

"How do you know who I'm looking for?"

"You're looking for Sal, aren't you?" He hadn't asked it as a question but a certain statement.

"How did you...."

"You have the same look on your face that you had when I asked you about him."

"Oh." She relaxed her face, no longer searching the crowd. She thought she would have finally got to meet him with it being her wedding day, but it didn't look like it was going to happen.

With the song ending and no one on the dance floor still, they exited as Angel approached.

"May I steal her?" Angel asked, looking at Drago.

"Sure." He immediately walked away, not even waiting for them to leave first, seeming to be distracted by something else.

Looks like the honeymoon phase of him being nice to me is over. Which was fine by her. She really wasn't prepared for the nice Drago, not knowing how to act around him.

"I want you to meet someone." Angel took her to a table full of people her age.

She wasn't there a second before a brunette practically jumped on her, giving her a hug.

Her brother smiled. "And this is Adalyn."

The girl just squeezed harder. "It's so nice to finally meet you, Kat."

Laughing, she wrapped her arms around her knowing this had to be the Caruso her brother was with. "It's nice to meet you too."

"You have to meet my friends," she said, finally letting her go. "This is my best friend, Lake."

The much taller brunette smiled. "Hi."

"Hi."

Adalyn then pointed to the strawberry blonde beside Lake. "And this is Elle."

A sweet Elle smiled too. "Hi, Chloe's told me a lot about you."

"You know Chloe?" Kat asked, taking an empty seat to get the weight of the dress off her.

Adalyn sat down too while Angel left to go talk with his brothers.

"Yeah, she's my best friend," the strawberry blonde told her.

Taking a look around, she saw Lucca but not her, making her realize she hadn't seen Chloe all night. "Where is she?"

Elle bit her lip clearly trying to think of what to say. "She couldn't make it."

"That's okay." Kat smiled, reassuring her it was no big deal.

When a seat was scooted back, Maria sat in it before she flipped her glass of champagne back. She seemed to be on edge.

"Something wrong?" Kat was the one to ask while the others just stared at her, watching her down the contents of the glass.

Maria set down the flute and waited a second before answering, "Yeah, no one's dancing."

"Once the alcohol gets into the Lucianos' systems, they will be," she revealed in a sarcastic tone that actually wasn't sarcastic at all. The Luciano family was rough and knew how to party hard.

She raised her brow. "They will?"

"Are they serving anything other than wine and champagne?" Kat had only noticed those drinking glasses around.

"Yes, it's a full open bar."

"Then give it thirty minutes," she said with certainty.

All the girls laughed.

She saw the tall, handsome blond who Drago had slammed the door on. He looked like he might be walking over here with another guy. "Who is that cute blond? He was the one who dropped off the pizza for us." She leaned over asking Maria.

What she had heard just a moment before wasn't laughter; now it was full-on laughter.

"That's my boyfriend, Vincent," Lake finally told her when she stopped.

"And my brother." Adalyn giggled.

Oops. "Sorry, I didn't kn—"

"It's okay," Lake stopped, her clearly unbothered. "He would get a kick out of it if he knew."

Maria, however, had yet to stop laughing. She practically had tears in her eyes.

She didn't understand what was so funny about it.

"What's so funny?" Vincent asked when he finally reached them.

Please don't! Please don't say anything.

Wiping away a tear, the princess flipped her hair over her shoulder. "Oh, nothing."

Lake smiled, playing dumb for her. "This is my boyfriend, Vincent."

"Hello, I think we've met." The tall, handsome blond dazzled his perfect teeth at her while holding his hand out.

"Y-Yes." She got stuck staring into his amazing baby blues. Pretty boys like him didn't exist in her world. Trying not to look like more of an idiot, she tried to get herself under control. "Hi, I'm Kat."

"It's good to meet you without a door in my face." He winked at her before going to stand next to his girl.

"And this is my boyfriend, Nero," Elle spoke, bringing her attention to the guy who had walked over with Vincent.

She looked at the other one. He had dark hair and emerald-green eyes. He was handsome as well, but to her it was very obvious that he was another brother of Lucca's. He resembled him in a lot of ways, not as scary looking, but he was still young, she supposed. "Hello."

Nero gave his hi with a simple nod as he stood close to Elle.

Yeah, definitely Lucca's brother.

With a song change, there seemed to be some brave, drunk souls that went out to the dance floor.

"Ooo, let's dance." The tall Lake stood, taking Elle's and Adalyn's hands.

On the way up, Adalyn grabbed Kat's. "Come dance with us."

Afraid of saying no to the girl, she looked back at Maria for help.

"I'll be there in a few." She made no effort of getting up but instead looked around the room for someone in particular.

"Hello, what about us?" a frustrated Vincent yelled out when he and Nero were left behind.

She was dragged to the dance floor by girls she had just met minutes ago, who made her feel welcome in their group as they started dancing. She wasn't that into it at first but slowly relaxed as she danced to the music, and it got a lot easier the more and more people came onto the dance floor after watching them having fun. The boys even joined their girlfriends, but it took longer for Angel to join his after several heated glances from Adalyn.

Steadily, the air in the room changed from a tense situation to an all-out carefree party. Who would've thought that a wedding and a lot of booze could've made these two families coexist in the same room at least for a one night?

She wasn't sure how long they had danced, but she was sweaty under the heavy dress when a slow song started, breaking the groups up into couples. Kat was heading to take a break when the handsomest Caruso came over.

"Would you like to dance?" Leo asked with a smile.

She couldn't help but smile back, taking the hand he was holding out to her. "It would be my pleasure."

"It looks like my son has taken to your wife." Dante sat down his whiskey glass, nodding to where the Luciano girl and Leo were dancing.

After their first dance, Drago had spent the night right beside his boss, not liking the air in the room. His instinct to protect his boss was just too strong, being an easy target in this room and in this situation. The Carusos were relying on fear to keep the Lucianos in line. However, the longer he sat protecting his boss, the more he had only watched her. His wife. It was as if he was becoming mesmerized by Katarina the longer he continued to watch her laugh and dance.

He thought the need for revenge would have been satiated. It had started to taste sweet when Dominic had met him before he walked down the aisle, but it quickly turned bitter with every look he glanced her way. She had spent their whole reception not with her family but with the Carusos, the little witch becoming even more and more likable. Ever since Leo had met her, Drago had spent days hearing him talk about her up until the wedding, and now she was dancing with him, making the kid happy. "I see that."

Dante raised his glass. "I couldn't have chosen better myself," he told him before taking a drink.

Fuck, even his boss was happy, which was sometimes a hard thing to accomplish.

But why wasn't *he*? Even after getting his revenge…

His boss could see he hadn't stopped watching her either. "Why don't you go dance with her?"

Taking his eyes off her, he finally scanned the room seeing only happy, drunk faces. "I'm not leaving you unprotected."

"I'm not unprotected. I have Todd and enough of my men around me."

Todd and the other Caruso men standing around the boss protecting him weren't Drago.

"Go dance with her," Dante ordered this time. "It'll make me and the families happy."

His eyes moved around the room once more seeing no threats,

so he nodded telling himself that he was going to dance with his wife, not because he wanted to but because he was following orders.

Men. They could be so stupid.

"May I steal her?"

She heard the words for the second time tonight, except this time it didn't come from her brother and instead from someone she didn't expect.

"I guess." Reluctantly, Leo let him have her to dance with.

"I think he wanted to finish the song." Kat laughed while she watched a sad Leo walk away.

Drago grabbed her waist before the kid could come back to take her away. "Too bad. He's not the one married to you."

Deciding to play along, she smiled as she raised a brow. "You're not jealous, are you?"

"Might be, if he were older."

She was stunned for a second. Hearing him say that didn't sound like the little game they were playing pretending to be husband and wife. That almost sounded real. *And why is he being nice again? What in the hell is in the air tonight?* Everyone in this whole damn room was getting along too nicely; it wasn't making sense. "Why is everyone so happy?" She didn't even realize the question had passed her lips till Drago answered her.

"Because it's a start to a new world, Katarina."

This time when she looked around, she could see it for what it really was… the beginning of peace. The Carusos had really called it; mixing their bloods could stop the possibility of war forever. With Angel and Adalyn, she and Drago, and the families safely interacting with each other, it opened up more relationship possibilities to a point where the families wouldn't dare to touch the other in fear their own could get hurt in the crossfire. It was genius.

Kat bit her lip. "I guess it's not so bad… marrying you, then."

"Yeah." His fire eyes stared down at the lip she'd just bit. "I suppose so."

"Kiss!" someone yelled out so loudly you could hear it over the music.

Her eyes now fell to his lips at the request.

"Kiss, kiss, kiss, kiss, kiss, kiss!" More and more people started to chant with a clap of their hands until everyone in the whole room was chanting and watching them, waiting on the edge of their seats for their first kiss.

Kat didn't know if it was the magic in the air, or if it was the excitement of the new world, but when Drago lifted her chin up with a finger, she parted her lips, closing her eyes. The lips that took hers were ones of possession, not of an equal marriage. That should have scared her, but there was no time as real fear was soon about to set in.

BANG.

Hearing the first shot sent the room to a quiet standstill.

It was only when a shrilling scream filled the room that people realized what they feared they'd heard was real. The second gunshot that was going to sound out soon enough was only going to confirm it.

With everyone in the room either screaming or running to take cover, it sent what was a lovely night of celebration to a twenty-first-century arranged marriage… straight from hell.

BANG.

THE END OF A BEAUTIFUL BEGINNING

Two would be shot.

One would survive.

One would be killed.

Both might just be the end to a beautiful beginning.

MAKING THEIR MARRIAGE THE SHORTEST ONE IN HISTORY

T*he second the first shot* rang out, Drago pulled his lips away from hers, hearing that shrilling scream that sent goose bumps up everyone's back. Before she knew it, he used the speed of a bullet dropping them to the ground.

His tall body lay over hers, protecting her as people started running and trampling over each other. "When I lift off you, you're going to crawl to that table in the corner."

Feeling her heart pumping, she didn't have time to answer before the pressure of his large body was lifted off her and she was forced to turn over and begin crawling with Drago's help with her heavy dress.

Once they reached the corner, Matthias found them, keeping low to the ground himself.

"Cover her," Drago ordered her brother.

Matthias reacted quickly, doing what he was asked.

Standing up, Drago flipped the long table that was holding their wedding cake, sending everything on it flying.

Taken aback at the sight of him, it took Kat a second before she and Matthias crawled behind the table that now sat on its side, putting it to their backs and using it as a shield.

At that time, the rest of the crew she was dancing with started to crawl over, with Nero bringing Elle over first, then Vincent with Lake.

Drago squatted down in front of them, taking the protection from the table, and grabbing the material at Kat's waist.

"What are you doing?!" she screamed at him when the poufy material of her outer layers was ripped off.

"In case you need to run." He continued, only leaving a couple of thin ones remaining.

Her mouth fell open already hearing the aftermath of all this. "Maria is going to fucking kill you."

He couldn't care less. "You do not move from behind this table unless you absolutely have to." Putting his sole focus on Matthias and looking him dead in the eyes, he ordered, "Do. Not. Let her out of your fucking sight. Got it?" He emphasized some of the words with even more severity.

"Got it." Her brother nodded sternly right when Angel got Adalyn safely behind the table.

This time Drago addressed all the men. "I don't want anyone moving from behind this table. You stay here and protect the women."

A fierce Nero, Vincent, and Angel nodded.

Satisfied by their responses, Drago stood again. The fire in his eyes burned to fevering heights as he started walking away from the safety he had created and into the chaos.

She and her two brothers stared at him in awe.

"Does he think he's the fucking Terminator?" Matthias asked, watching Drago leave them without at least crouching down, uncaring if the shooter decided to strike out again.

The Carusos with them, however, weren't surprised one bit by him, but it was Nero who responded simply, with fire in his green-emerald eyes as well. "That's because he is."

It was then she felt the liquid that coated the front of her dress right over her heart. Pulling her hand away, she saw thick, deep-red blood staining her hand.

"M-M-Matthias...." She finally got his name out, her heart thumping faster and faster, trying to work harder and harder.

"Kat!" he cried out, seeing the blood on her hands while he quickly touched her chest trying to find where it came from in order to apply pressure. "Where are you hurt?!"

Angel and the rest of them became just as fearful and grabbed to help her.

Her heart finally stopped.... "It isn't mine."

Drago had felt it the second the bullet had pierced through his arm. It had been a kill shot that only missed the target because he had put his body in front of hers at just the right moment.

Someone had intentions to kill Katarina, almost making their marriage the shortest one in history. That might have been a plus to him before they'd been married, but now that she was his wife and she had almost died in his arms, he couldn't get the image out of his head of what would have happened to her if his instincts hadn't kicked in to protect her.

Now that they were married—regardless if they wanted to be or not—she was his, and if someone threatened what was his, he took it personally and… someone had hell to fucking pay.

It had taken everything he had to leave her in her brothers' trust, knowing he could only guarantee protection in his own hands, but he had others to protect as well. He had been doing this too long, knowing full and well that first shot that had been fired… had found its target.

It was the way that woman had screamed. She wasn't the one who had been shot. He knew the difference between a cry for help from a victim and a cry for help from someone who'd witnessed it. The witness always screamed louder, and he feared she had seen the worst.

That bullet had taken a soul with it.

"It's his blood." She felt her heart start back up again with the pounding. "It's D-Drago's blood."

"He'll be fine," Nero reassured her with confidence.

This feeling of worry for him rushed over her. She didn't know why it was there, but the fact remained, it was there. "How do you know?"

Vincent wasn't worried in the slightest. "I would be surprised if that bastard even felt it."

Kat looked at the handsome blond like he was crazy. "He got shot!"

"He's been shot lots of times," Vincent told her with a shrug. "You know how he got shot five times?"

She rolled her eyes starting to understand why the door got slammed in his face. "Yes, I'm aware my father tried to have him killed."

"Well, he didn't go down till the fifth one."

"Oh." That was the part she hadn't heard, and she understood why he had brought it up now. "Really?"

Angel was the one who answered, "He's right."

She strangely looked over to him wondering how he knew that.

"Lucca has a tape of it. I asked him to show me."

"He'll be okay, Kat." Adalyn and the rest of the girls who were being smothered by their men started reassuring her as well.

"Cassius!" She grabbed her youngest brother's hand, jerking him down when he found them all behind the table. "Are you crazy? Get down!" This was going to be another conversation she was going to have with him about fear.

Cassius looked at her in-between trying to peer out. "Your husband is badass."

Oh God. "Did you see him. Was he okay?"

"Yeah, I saw him chasing after some guy right after he flipped this whole fucking table over." Clearly, he had been just as much as in awe as they had.

"Did you see who it was?" Angel asked.

"No, I didn't get a good look after everyone started running." Cassius glanced out again.

"Stop it." She tried to keep him down this time using the bloody hand.

Cassius' face turned serious when he saw her covered in blood. "Are you hurt?"

"No, but I think Drago is…."

The serious expression quickly vanished, returning back to his usual self as he tried to take a peek again. When Kat didn't let him, he revealed something else. "It's safe to look. There's no one doing anything. It's a standoff right now."

Matthias, Angel, Nero, and Vincent quickly glanced up to take a look after what Cassius had said, all of them giving a collective, "Oh fuck."

Kat's eyes went two times the size. She had a feeling she knew what they meant by that.

Lake was the only one brave one to ask, "What is it?"

"Well…," Vincent began, opening his beautiful but big mouth. "It's exactly what he said… a fucking standoff between the families."

THE MAN WHO HAD MET HIS UNTIMELY END

O*n one side, the Carusos* stood, and on the other, the Lucianos, as they all held out their weapons staring the other family down.

"They killed one of ours," one of the Caruso men yelled out, ready to pull the trigger.

Everyone behind the table looked at each other. Nero and Vincent stared at her twin brothers a little harder with a scrutinizing gaze.

"Our men wouldn't have shot anywhere near my sister," Angel hissed at the two, and knowing he was right, unlike the rest of the Carusos, they no longer scrutinized them.

Leaving only one question between them. Which Caruso had fallen?

What if it's. . . She made herself not say her new husband's name in her head. *I'm sure he's fine.*

"How do we know you didn't accidentally kill one of your own?" a Luciano yelled back.

"Because we're Carusos. We don't kill our own." A different Caruso spoke up, referencing the new Luciano boss, who'd let his own father get murdered to save the family.

Dominic stepped into the middle of no-man's-land without fear, jumping on a table to stand and look down on all the men in the room. "We came without guns like I promised." His voice commanded the room, demanding attention from every soul. "You checked every one of my men on the way in."

The Caruso men's eyes scanned, only seeing small knives and anything they could get ahold of to use as a weapon.

"Dante, call your men down." He spoke louder, his voice traveling farther, calling out the other head of the family to step out. "So we can deal with this man to man." However, the Luciano boss wasn't done. He spun on the table to only look down and address his family with a threat. "And if it was one of my men who defied my orders, then I will hand him over to you myself."

The Caruso boss finally rose, coming into focus with an unforgiving face that looked like he wanted to see every Luciano man, woman, and child dead. He opened his mouth to give an order when the ballroom doors flung open and a furious Drago walked through.

Drago walked straight to his boss, quietly whispering to him what he knew. Whatever it was only made his boss look more confused and unhappier.

It appeared Dante was beginning to have a change of heart

after their conversation, but the boss didn't say anything, clearly still contemplating how he wanted to proceed.

"He's going to make his men step down, right?" Kat asked, looking at Nero, knowing full well they were father and son.

Nero didn't say anything, his emerald-colored eyes still fiercely glowing. It looked like he was about to defy Drago's orders to protect Elle when the ballroom doors opened once more, making him stay right where he was after seeing who entered.

Lucca walked through, seeming to be in the same state as Drago, a bit out of breath and sweaty like the two had been running. Except he hadn't entered as the Caruso underboss, but the boogieman.

She had seen him in the all black suit earlier, thinking he somehow looked more dangerous than usual, but now he looked absolutely fucking terrifying.

Lucca didn't even look to the boss, giving out his own orders without consulting his father. "Put your guns down," he ordered his men with a voice so deadly that not only his men put down their guns, but the Lucianos lowered their weapons out of fear.

With the threat of an almost war breaking out, Drago's eyes went to the table they were hiding behind until they fell on hers, peeking out from behind it.

"Is he coming over here?" she asked, seeing him start to walk their way.

"I think so," Adalyn told her before glancing over at her to give her a sympathetic look.

"I don't like the way he's fucking looking at her," Matthias said and looked at the other end of the table to his twin.

"Me either," Elle admittedly whispered.

Lake reached over to pat her hand. "It's going to be a rough night for you, sweetie."

Kat swallowed as she hunkered down behind the table, no longer able to watch the bodyguard stalk closer.

"Fuck that." Adalyn moved closer to her. "We need to all protect her. We can't keep letting these men run over us."

Nodding, Lake moved closer to her as well. "Where the hell is Maria with her Louboutins when you need her?"

When sweet Elle tried to move closer, Nero grabbed her, keeping her right where she was, daring her with his eyes not to try it.

By the time Drago reached her, the tense air in the group only got tenser when he saw them blocking him from her.

"Fuck this. It has nothing to do with us." Vincent quickly grabbed Lake back, realizing Nero had known best.

The handsome blond quickly got demoted to just cute for her.

"If you really thought I would ever hurt her, you wouldn't have let me marry her." He addressed her brothers who were protecting her in seriousness before he changed back, becoming angry again. "Now, you have five seconds to move away from *my wife.*"

"Yep. Okay." Matthias quickly agreed, backing up along with his two other brothers and Angel grabbing a still protective Adalyn. They didn't only agree because they knew Drago could crush them with his foot after what they had seen, but because they knew what he had said was true. Tonight had even proven that. They'd watched him get her to safety.

"What the—!" Katarina was snatched up as Drago threw her in her torn-up dress over his shoulder. He was getting her the fuck out of there, not trusting her to come with him if he let her walk, when the arguing between the two families started up again, but at least this time weapons weren't being used.

Seeing Dom, she almost yelled out for help, but then she saw Lucca with him, both of them staring down at a man who lay flat on his back, lifeless on the floor. Having the advantage of the view of being on his shoulders, she saw it then, the bullet hole that sat right between his eyes.

Oh God.

Bile was rising in her throat as she recognized the dead Caruso.

Her eyes flew back to the boogieman and saw an unremorseful expression, like he couldn't have fucking cared less his man was dead.

"Did you find who did this?" she asked Drago the question, not knowing if she really wanted the answer.

Drago slightly adjusted her on his shoulder before he gruffed out the answer. "No. I lost him."

Chills coated every inch of her skin as she watched Lucca get farther and farther away in the distance. She remembered how the underboss wasn't there to be found in the room during the standoff and had conveniently come back after Drago.

The exact words she had used the last time she had seen the Caruso alive came back to her mind… *Well, he'll be dead soon.*

She whispered the name of the man who had met his untimely end, "Todd."

BULLET HOLES FROM MY FATHER

D*rago threw her in her* gown onto his bed. "You're going to stay right here, and you may not leave this apartment unless I say so, do you understand?"

"W-Why?" She stared up at the fierce man.

He didn't sugarcoat it. "Because someone tried to kill you."

"How do you kno— Are you okay?!" Her mindset quickly changed as he pulled off his black suit jacket that was hiding his white stained button-up shirt underneath.

Taking a seat on the bed beside her, he was beginning to reveal the tiredness he actually felt. "I'll be fine," he assured her, starting to unbutton his shirt to access the wound and placing the bloody shirt on the floor. "It's just a graze."

"A graze?!" She looked at his arm, seeing a chunk of skin missing

"Yes, now, can you go into the bathroom and hand me the first aid kit under the sink and a towel?"

Getting up, she quickly gathered the bottom of her dress that still remained before going into the bathroom, grabbing the kit, and taking a towel from the hanger.

After she returned, Drago took the towel from her first, draping it over himself, and then the kit, opening it and pulling out a bottle of alcohol. Carefully, he poured some of the liquid over the wound, washing some of the blood away.

Watching him do that to himself without even making a sound, she found herself awestruck again before she finally snapped out of it. "I-I can help." Kat grabbed the alcohol pad to help clean the area, not touching him till Drago gave her a nod. She began wiping the wound and getting the blood that was starting to dry off the area.

Not liking the quietness while she was tending to him, she asked him another grave question. "What makes you think he wanted to kill me?"

"Because whoever it is doesn't miss."

She stopped wiping and focusing on the wound to look at him. "Why do you say that?"

His voice became just as grave as her questions. "He's killed two of our men now, both times right between the eyes. He shoots to kill and doesn't miss."

"Well, he did tonight...."

"Only because I moved at just the right time, Katarina," he told her with force, knowing full-heartedly he was right. "I just don't get one thing..."

She licked her dry lip. The pounding in her chest started back up again.

"Why he went for your heart."

Going back to wiping with a shaky hand, she could no longer stare into his fiery eyes. It wasn't until she wiped away the last of the blood that she made a joke to hide the fear in her voice. "Poetic justice."

Drago's brows drew together. "Why would you say that?"

"Aren't those bullet holes from my father?" She couldn't help it when her eyes drifted to the five scars that marked his chest, one of them so close to his heart, she wondered if he would have said it was just a graze as well. "I suppose it would have been poetic, especially on our wedding day."

"I need to go." He quickly grabbed the white bandage, slapping it on his arm, then wrapping it with tape. Clearly, what she had told him made some sort of sense, even if it was only a joke.

She looked at him like he was crazy. "I think you need to rest."

However, he didn't listen to her and stood up.

Her eyes went wide when he towered over her, seeing him in all his bare-chested glory. She could safely say he was the biggest man she had ever seen... *Wait, is he bigger than the last time I saw him?*

She watched him go to a closet and pull out another shirt, her wandering eyes unable to look away to see all the scars the man carried. It was quite frightening, to be honest. Afraid for him, since he really didn't seem to know when to stop, she tried again. "You really don't look so good, Drago."

"I've been worse," he assured her.

"Where are you going that's so important?"

He put on his black jacket to cover up the blood that was starting to stain the shirt again; it concealed the wound like it wasn't even there. "I need to speak with Lucca."

"Did you happen to see Lucca when you were chasing the shooter down?"

He shook his head, beginning to leave. "No, he must have been going a different way."

Her heart raced yet again as she put out her hand, placing it on his good arm to stop him. She couldn't believe she was saying the next words that came out of her mouth, but she did. "Do you trust Lucca?"

He looked down on her. The fire that had slightly burned out in his eyes returned but was flaming brighter. "Why the fuck would you ask me that?"

"I-I—" Seeing his defensive response, she wasn't sure how to fix it, so instead of making something up, she decided to tell him the truth. She had seen something good in him tonight, and her opinion of him of not having a heart was slightly changing. She could only hope he showed her mercy for what she was about to say. "Because he scares the hell out of me."

That ring of fire calmed as a smile touched his lips. Taking her chin with his hand, he positioned her face up to him. Making it obvious that he liked she didn't care for Lucca.

She didn't know why she didn't move as he brought his face down closer to hers, but she stayed deathly still, finding herself anticipating the kiss.

Before his lips could touch hers, he stopped, his voice giving her lips the only caress they were about to get. "He should, Kat."

When Drago pulled away and started to disappear, she didn't know who she felt more betrayed by, herself... or him.

"Your things you packed are there," he continued, pointing to the small pile of boxes by the door as he passed. "And in case you missed him, there's a guard by the elevator."

The warning he gave her, she understood loud and clear that he didn't want her to leave the apartment. She went to open her mouth to protest, but he was already on the other side of the door, seconds away from closing it.

"Goodbye, Kat."

Hearing him say that again, she realized it was the first time he used her nickname, and she started to really fucking hate that she liked the way it sounded when he said it.

LUCIFER'S MARK

K*atarina went through her boxes* trying to find the ones that held what she needed for tonight. She supposed she could have started to unpack, but then that would have made all of this come true, that she was really living here now.

Grabbing fresh clothes and her toiletries, she used his bathroom and took a quick shower to remove the blood off her. When she came out freshly cleaned and clothed, she took her shambles of a wedding dress with her, not knowing how she was supposed to break the news to Maria that the couture wedding dress was ruined. She found the trash can and threw it in.

May she never know of the loss.

Knowing her, she'd be more upset over the dress than over Todd.

Not ready for bed just yet, she couldn't help herself from doing a bit of snooping. She wanted to know more of the man she was up against. The stairs had been calling her name since the first time she'd been here. Heading to them, she placed one foot on the step when something caught her eye.

Taking her foot off, she went back, going to the one lonely picture that hung on his wall that she had missed.

It was a photo of the Caruso boss and his children, but in the back stood Drago crossing his arms. Except this Drago didn't look quite like the one who had just left. The one in the photo had a much bigger presence.

That was when she was fully able to see what her father had done to him, besides the holes he'd left on his chest.

She could see the muscle mass he once had was gone. His beautiful Italian dark skin now had a gray tint, the deep bags he carried under his eyes didn't use to be there, and the biggest change she could see was in his eyes. They used to hold less of a red color, being more brownish, but closing her eyes, she pictured them how they'd shone earlier, red rings of fire that were hellbound.

Lucifer hadn't put him in a coma; he had sent him to hell, and those eyes had seen the abyss.

Her father had always left scars on his victims, but what he'd loved the most was the change he made in a person's eyes after he had broken them. She called it… Lucifer's mark.

Kat could always see it, like the way she had with Chloe, but she had missed it this time, like she had only one time before…

. . .Still crying behind the door, she heard it go deathly quiet until footsteps got closer and closer to the basement door. Spending most of her ten-year-old life behind this door, she had learned whose footsteps were whose, and the ones coming closer belonged to the devil.

Quickly, she ran down the steps, but the second she was three steps away from the bottom, a hand came out, shoving her to the concrete basement floor.

With everything going fuzzy, she tried to fight it, crawling on the cold ground in hopes to get away.

"No!" Dominic yelled. His young broken body had fallen down the steps, but being the strongest of the brothers and already withstanding the beating he and the twins had taken to protect her, he was the only one still capable as he righted himself trying to grab the man who was coming after her.

"You can't fucking protect her from me this time," Lucifer spat before he gave him the back of his hand across his face, sending him to the ground with his sister. It had been awhile since he had gotten ahold of her, and he was itching to do it again.

When Dom tried to get up to fight again, Lucifer kicked him repeatedly wherever he felt so fit.

Kat made it under the bed to a tiny space below the mattress being held up by an old rusty frame. She watched her brother get kicked over and over again through the tears in her eyes.

Their father finally stopped hitting Dominic at a brutal place in between no longer being able to move and right before losing consciousness. Whatever the devil was about to do, he wanted Dominic to witness it.

She looked at Dominic's hazel eyes. They were still resilient, but with every step Lucifer took toward her, they got closer to the verge of breaking. Now watching the shoes get closer and closer, she screamed as a hand came down, snatching a handful of her hair.

The pain she felt at her scalp from being dragged out from under the bed was unbearable, but it wasn't going to compare to what came next... If there was a devil, there must have been a god, because thankfully, she didn't last through the pain, passing out after only a couple of blows.

One thing about their father was, he got no enjoyment if he couldn't see their eyes, wanting to see the fear in them as he broke them.

What Kat missed, however, was that when Dominic could finally crawl his damaged body to her small unconscious one, he scooped her up, holding her like he had when she was a baby.

After twenty long years of Lucifer's torture and being unbreakable... he had finally broken, and the devil wasn't even there to see it...

...Like Drago, she didn't find out her brother had broken till later, and when she did, she realized they were a very different type of broken. It was the kind of broken like when breaking a bone, except when a bone heals, the part where it broke becomes stronger.

Trying to hold back the tear that was threatening to fall, she felt something on the other side of the picture. Turning it over, she read the words on a piece of paper that had been taped on the back.

Happy Birthday, Drago. Love, Leo.

She smiled, able to see the full Drago. He had a heart after all. Turning the picture over, she was going to place it back on the wall when she noticed a face she hadn't seen at first glance, because she'd focused solely on Drago.

The tear she had been holding in fell, splashing onto the photo over the face that held the blackish-blue eyes.

Sal.

I HATE YOU FOR THIS

D*rago only knocked once before* entering Lucca's office hoping he was in here, expecting to find the boss or maybe the consigliere with him, but what he didn't expect was Maria.

"What are you doing in here?" he asked.

She just raised a brow. "Todd was pretty much my personal bodyguard, or have you already forgotten?"

Not in the mood for her antics, he focused on what he came for and sat down in front of his underboss. "One-Shot tried to kill Katarina."

Lucca, who had been eerily quiet dragging on his cigarette and was in his own little world thinking, suddenly snapped out of it. "What did you say?"

"He tried to kill Katarina." The words came out harsher the second time. "He missed her heart by a second."

Pulling the cigarette away from his lips, he furrowed his brows. "One-Shot doesn't miss."

Drago took of his jacket, revealing his bullet wound. "Technically, he didn't."

Lucca sat back in his chair now, taking a couple of hits just staring at the blood on the sleeve of the button-up shirt. "He didn't go for the head," he stated, seeming to already know the killer hadn't.

"No, her heart."

"Fitting," Maria mumbled.

Looking over at her, he assumed the girls must be on the right track. "Kat used the words 'poetic justice.'"

"Seems to me One-Shot is into the theatrics." She couldn't help but comment again, "Not only did he kill a Caruso, but he tried for a Luciano… just like last time when he killed one of ours, he went for a Luciano, only he was successful last time."

The room went quiet as Lucca inhaled deeply. Something seemed to click for him. "He's evening the score."

Every instinct in Drago's body went on high alert telling him of the danger to come. "Except this time it's not even."

The underboss nodded. "We will need to keep a close eye on Katarina and warn Angel to be careful. I will talk with Dominic, so he knows one of his men is next, but I'm sure he's figured it out by now."

All their heads turned when the office door opened, and a concerned Sal walked in. "I think we may have a problem."

The room went eerily quiet. The smoke from Lucca's cigarette moving through the space seemed to make the most noise.

"I have no visual of One-Shot entering or leaving the casino hotel."

"How is that possible?" Drago was the one to ask.

Sal was a man who knew everything. He was the great Salvatore, for Christ's sake. However, this day he didn't, and you could see the frustration etched on his face. "I'm not sure yet."

"Well, he didn't appear out of fucking thin air."

Deep in thought, Lucca seemed to snap out of it at Drago's words. "Just keep looking."

Sal nodded but didn't leave the room. It was like a dark shadow casted over him, his voice becoming grave. "I don't have a good feeling about this, Lucca. And I got this eerie feeling that *he's*. . . ."

It was the boogieman who finished the sentence. "One of *us*."

He knew what that meant. Everyone in the room did. It had been in the back of each one of their minds that One-Shot might not be a Luciano after all, but a Caruso. Which was the worst outcome of all, because not only would they have to put down a brother, but that meant none of them or their loved ones were safe. This wouldn't have been such a problem for Drago a day ago, but now that he was married, it was becoming a bigger fucking problem by the second. He'd protected so many throughout his life, but the protectiveness he was beginning to feel was somehow different. So different it scared him, and he didn't understand why he was feeling this way after only a few hours of being married to the little witch.

He stood up. The big man towered over them. "Katarina will need to be a priority."

"Like I said, we will keep a close eye on her," his underboss agreed. "But I need your help in finding One-Shot."

"You will, and when I find him, I'm going to put a fucking bullet through his heart." Staring down at Lucca intensely, he never wanted to wring his underboss's neck until now. "You know I hate you for this, right?"

Maria slightly tilted her head.

Putting the butt of the stick to his mouth, he inhaled deeply, staring up at his man with the same intensity. "For what?"

"For choosing me to marry her."

Lucca stood then, his cool-colored eyes burning into warm-colored ones. "I showed you her. I didn't pick her, Drago. You did."

And that he did.

Going for the door, he turned before he walked out, wanting to know one last thing. "But you knew I wouldn't be able to resist her though, didn't you?"

That twisted smile he always seemed to miss on Lucca appeared on his lips. "That I did."

Fucker.

Looking at her nude nails to see if there were any imperfections, she spoke when the room was just theirs. "I thought he might have killed you there for a second, brother. You better be careful, or the little games you've been playing might get you killed."

"That's where you're wrong." He flicked his Zippo open over

and over again. "I'm not playing games."

She looked at Lucca. "Then what exactly are you doing?"

"Creating our future for when this city is mine."

Maria stood, getting up from the leather couch that sat in his office to sit in the chair in front of his desk. "Nothing is set in stone, so what makes you so sure you get to have the throne?"

"There're only two people smart enough to take it from me," he began, rolling the Zippo through his fingers. "Dominic is the first, and if he's not careful, I'll have to take care of him."

She crossed her legs, sitting up straighter at the confession before she cleared her throat. "And the other?"

He stopped the metal in his hands from moving, coming to a standstill. "Is sitting right in front of me."

Seeing his eyes bore into hers, she gave him a smile. "Good thing for you, your men wouldn't follow orders from a woman, let alone into hell like they would you."

"And you're sure Todd… didn't?" he asked coldly.

That smile of hers slowly disappeared. She figured he would find out that Todd had taken her to get Katarina's wedding dress, but she wondered if he knew that they had gone to the Lucianos' house first. "Good thing I know killing someone with a bullet is no fun for you, or I'd be tempted into thinking you were One-Shot."

"Todd was a dead man." The boogieman confirmed that he would have killed him for his carelessness. "But I need Katarina alive. She serves a purpose for me."

That smile that had disappeared from Maria's lips returned.

"You know

I've been thinking about what we should do with Amo… and I might just have an idea."

AMO DE SANTIS

Knock.

The single knock on the door had his blue-green gaze going to the wooden door. "Come in." When the door opened and the young but large man came through to take a seat in front of him, he didn't avert his eyes once, always showing him exactly what he truly felt about him. "I have a job for you, Amo."

He sat there like a cold statue, not saying a word or making a movement. There was never any emotion on his face anymore, always showing the same stoic face Amo had ever since he'd lost Chloe to Lucca.

"An attempt on Drago's wife, Katarina, was made tonight by One-Shot." He waited to see Amo's reaction to the news to see if there was any remorse or concern, but there was still nothing. "And I am requesting that you be her personal bodyguard whenever Drago is not around."

Finally something, a little flash in his eyes of what appeared to be hatred before a simple nod was given.

Lucca flicked his Zippo open, revealing a flame to light the end of a cigarette he held between his lips. "That won't be a problem, will it?"

"No, sir." It was the first words he had spoken to him in a long time.

Unable to hold the words in any longer, the underboss whispered to him, revealing what he had known and what Amo thought he had gotten away with. "Does Angel know it was you?"

A hidden fear that was probably even hidden to Amo started to creep into his eyes. "What?"

"Don't play dumb with me, Amo." His voice became harsh and quick. "Does Angel know it was you who beat the shit out of him?"

Amo's mouth opened before it snapped closed. He was clearly thinking about his next words before he spoke the truth simply with a word. "Yes."

Good. So, he wants me to deal with him.

Placing his still lit cigarette in the glass ashtray, Lucca slowly stood, taking in right where he had Amo trapped as he walked to the other side of the desk and took a seat on the edge, so he could look down upon him. "I want you to know if I thought for one second you were One-Shot or had the ability to hurt a Luciano again, I would slit your throat right here and now and finally be fucking done with you... But I know you are not." The boogieman started to rise with the cold words he spoke next. "Because you are weak. Too weak to carry a skill such as One-Shot's and too weak to kill even if your life depended on it. You covered your face with a mask in hopes to hide your identity from a man you thought to be weaker than you even though it took three of you to take him down. When you hurt someone..."

Lucca stood once more, this time reaching out to grab Amo's thick neck as he started to squeeze the life out of him. "You do so like this. Face to face. A Caruso never hides behind a mask. Those are for the weak." Even though Amo was beginning to struggle for air and tried to fight him off, Lucca continued with his strong grip and words, "There is so much more joy to be had when there is nothing to hide behind as you watch life leave their eyes."

Finally, his grip left his neck as Amo fought for air, but he didn't yet relieve him of his scolding. "Until I release you, you will spend every day of your foreseeable future protecting the Luciano girl, the sister of the ones you hate so much. Do you understand?"

Holding his neck, he got his breathing back under control. "Yes, sir."

Lucca went back to his desk and picked up the cigarette that was still lit. "You are dismissed," he said before taking a long hit.

It took a moment for Amo to collect himself before he stood. Instead of walking out, he had something to ask, "Does Drago know?"

"No," he answered, gravely seeing that he'd learned nothing of the last few minutes they'd shared. Amo was still afraid of removing that mask and revealing his crimes he had committed to his uncle. *Still weak.*

Amo went to leave, but it wasn't before Lucca bestowed his

wisdom on him once more.

"If anything happens to her in your care, it won't be the Luciano brothers you will be answering to; it will be your uncle. You will come to find out he has grown quite fond of Katarina. Even if it was her father, Lucifer, who tried to kill him. Drago is coming to find forgiveness but… will you?"

Watching Amo walk out the door, he didn't think that day would ever come by seeing the hatred he had built up in his eyes of everyone and everything. Amo De Santis had the right to hate only one person in the world, and that was Lucca himself. It wasn't until he'd seen the hate he'd built for Chloe that he wanted the young man dead.

But everyone, even the ones he despised, *has a part to play in the war.*

KITTY KAT

"A *part of me always hoped* One-Shot was you," Lucca spoke through the phone, "Dominic."

The Luciano boss was very silent on the other end of the phone.

"But it looks like you're not the only one who possess the skills that you have with a gun and a bullet in the chamber."

He had to of been glad to hear his name was in the clear but it was obvious Dominic got the feeling that something bad might have happened for that. "What makes you finally say that?"

"Oh, you haven't heard?"

"Heard what?" his voice demanded to know.

Figuring he had been busy the last couple of hours with his men, Lucca told the enemy what cleared his name for good. "He went for

Katarina."

Dominic went silent again on the other end for several moments before he threatened the scariest man in all of Kansas City. "I don't give a fuck who you are, Lucca Caruso. If something happens to my sister in your possession, I promise you, you'll be the first one I'll kill. Never forget it was you who promised me her protection, and you will have to answer for your sins."

If he hadn't promised exactly that to him, he would make the Luciano pay for that threat, but since he did, and it was his sister, he would let it slide. *For now.* "Katarina is safer here than with you."

"And how is that?" he asked in frustration.

"Because she has one thing here that you don't..." Lucca paused only for a second. "Drago."

Quietly, he entered the apartment after getting his bullet wound stitched up to see the pink-haired girl sleeping peacefully on his bed. By the time he took a shower and dressed, and the early morning light was shining through, she was still fast asleep.

Wishing they had discussed their sleeping arrangements earlier, he found his eyes wandering between the empty space beside her and the cold leather couch. Taking a seat on the empty side of the edge of the bed, he decided there was *no way in hell* he was sleeping on his couch in his apartment.

It must have been guilt to make Drago glance back at her one last time before he got up, taking a pillow with him to the couch.

There were many things he didn't know about Katarina yet, and many things she didn't know about him. With her father being the devil and seeing perhaps a glimpse of the abuse she might have suffered at his hand, he didn't feel comfortable with her waking up next to man she didn't even know. Regardless if she was his wife, there needed to at least be a discussion before he would lie in the same bed with her, even to just sleep.

He adjusted the pillow under his head and tried to get his well over six-foot body frame comfortable on the couch. It made you think maybe chivalry wasn't dead after all.

That little witch will be sleeping on the couch from now on.

Never mind.

Waking up the next day groggy in a different bed than she was used to was definitely strange, to say the least. Letting her eyes adjust to the light from the huge window, she had to rub them to see if she really was seeing the giant man sleeping on the couch in what looked like a horrible position. His head was craned onto one of the arms, and his feet were dangling off the other end. She felt bad for the poor soul when he would wake up, and she wondered if she should try and wake him up to move him to the bed... *Nah, he'll be fine.*

To her surprise, he hadn't woken up once, probably due to exhaustion from the night. However, that was about to quickly end as she opened the door to Angel.

Coming into the apartment, Angel set down the most important last things she owned. "How are you doing?"

"Good," she assured him knowing he and her brothers were probably worried, but she did so in a whisper, not wanting to wake the big sleeping baby.

His eyes searched the room then to see why she whispered. When he found Drago had slept on the couch, her brother's happiness was evident by the smug smile he held before he left the apartment as quietly as he'd entered.

Excited, Katarina went for what she'd been waiting for…

"What the fuck is that?"

Running her fingers along the black fur, she didn't pay attention to Drago's half-asleep voice.

Jumping up from the couch, he looked like he saw a demon in the house. "I said, what the fuck is that?!"

"Shadow," she answered, still petting the slick black fur as it rubbed up against her. "My cat."

Almost exactly on cue, Shadow meowed.

"You have got to be shitting me." He stared at them both now like they were possessed creatures of the night. "I knew you were a fucking witch."

"Excuse me?" Kat looked at him now like he was crazy.

"You heard me, witch. Your name is Kat, who has a cat that's fucking black, for Christ's sake, and you gave it a fucking creepy-ass name like Shadow. Why didn't you just call it Satan?" he said not so sarcastically and almost irate as he went to the fridge to grab a protein shake and downed the contents. "That thing ain't staying here."

"It's not a thing; it's a he, and his name is Shadow, and he's not going anywhere."

"Well, I was not told about a fucking cat. That is not what I signed up for."

"Well—" Kat's voice rose to match his as she stalked toward the big dumbass. "I didn't sign up for any of this. You picked me, asshole. It wasn't the other way around. I never wanted to get married not only to you, but ever, yet here we are making sacrifices for the greater good." She stalked even closer, pointing her pale finger till it reached his chest, and she poked it with every word that came out of her mouth next. "Now, if you would like to stay married to me, then Shadow stays. If not, give me the divorce papers and sign 'em, so I can give them to Lucca to tell him it was you who wanted out of this scam of a marriage over a little cat."

Pushing his chest deeper into her finger, he pushed her back till she was up against the kitchen island and planted against him. "You're going to really wish you didn't poke the bear, Kitty Kat, you really will."

Her breath hung in her throat for that five-point-four seconds, his fiery eyes delved deep into hers as his strong warm body covered hers, but then it disappeared right before a silent promise was made that she might have just fucked up.

Heading to the coat closet, he pulled out a suit before going to his dresser in the open space, then ripped out the rest of what he was going to wear. "This marriage isn't no scam, sweetheart. It's fucking real," he told her before tearing off his shirt, then his sleeping pants he had worn only for her.

Kat turned around quickly but not quickly enough not to see his ass cheeks before she did. "What are you doing? There's a fucking window right there, and all of Kansas City see your jun—"

"I don't give a fuck. This is how I get dressed every morning, and at night I sleep naked, and from now on, *I will* be sleeping in my bed with or without you." Quickly getting dressed, he continued to speak carefully. "We're married now, so get used to it. Only way you're getting rid of me is through death, and I don't plan on dying anytime soon."

Knock.

"Just in time," he gruffed after lacing his shoe.

Every bone in her body went limp wanting to scream bloody murder at the man, but instead, she just watched the now cleanly dressed man get up and open the door to someone she didn't recognize but was also a giant like Drago. However, this one was younger.

"This is my nephew." He brought him inside, closing the door. "Amo."

Amo just stared at her blankly, almost emotionless.

"Amo, this is Katarina." He nodded toward the stunned pink-haired woman whom he'd called witch only moments ago. "Not sure if you two met at the wedding, but this is my new, loving wife."

She stalked toward the bastard after hearing that sarcastic tone again at his last words. *That's it!*

Drago, however, caught her before she could do anything and leaned down to place a deep, long, and unforgiving kiss on her lips that sent her body back to the limp mode she was in before. "Don't wait up for me, sweetheart."

Staring at the door that he had just walked through with a smile and what seemed like a pep in his step, she had never felt more calm rage in her life. Then suddenly, her new goal in life hit her like a thousand pounds of bricks, and she knew what she would become....

A black widow.

WHAT'S MINE IS YOURS

"*It's nice to meet you.*" She smiled at him. "But why exactly are you here?"

It didn't seem like Amo really wanted to talk, but eventually he answered her, "I'll be watching over you."

"O-Okay." This was going to be weird, but she figured it was because of her almost getting shot through the heart that they were taking this precaution. He was Drago's nephew, after all, so he couldn't be that bad.

"Do you have a cell phone?"

"Yes." Of course, she had one. It was as cheap and slow as they came this day and age, but she did.

Snapping his finger, he held out his hand.

Quickly, she went to retrieve it from the pile of her things, pulling it out of the bag that she had placed her clothes in that she was wearing before the wedding. It was dead as a doornail when she handed it to him.

That, however, didn't much matter when he pulled the back cover off, taking out the sim card and breaking it right in two.

"What the hell was that for?!"

He ignored her and went to the trashcan, throwing the whole thing away.

"EXCUSE ME?!" Kat walked after him, frustrated and shocked at what he had the audacity to do.

"That thing was a piece of shit anyways," he told her before pulling out a brand-new shiny phone that was as good as it got and handing it to her. "It has any contacts you need in it."

Taking the phone, she had half a mind *to shove it up his ass,* but unlocking it and seeing how much better it was than what she had, she didn't want to part with it. "You could have handed me the new phone first, you know."

Amo shrugged before going to the fridge to see what they had. When he pulled out a protein shake, Kat could only roll her eyes, reminding her of her irritating new husband.

We're married now, so get used to it. She remembered him saying the harsh words and the display he gave her that only made her want to get back at him. Thinking about how to do that, she moved her eyes around the room till an idea finally hit her. *Then I guess what's mine is yours now.*

Going through her phone, she saw the name she was looking for right on top. She dialed it, and it wasn't long before it was answered and she heard the word, "Hello."

Kat smiled. "I need some help."

When they quickly hung up, Amo looked at her right after he finished the shake. Wanting to know, he asked, "Who was that?"

However, the one she'd called turned out to probably be just steps away. A knock sounded on the door.

Opening the door, she smiled when her brother Angel entered.

After having been there not long ago, he drew his brows together when he saw Amo standing in the kitchen. "What are you doing here?"

Kat didn't know what it was, but the air in the room suddenly changed as the two seemed to stare each other down.

"I was given *orders* to protect her," he said, clearly enunciating a particular word that meant something to Angel.

Not only Kat, but it looked like Amo was also concerned about what Angel was about to say next from the stern expression on his face, but then it passed. "All right." Looking back to his sister, he seemed to cool down to his usual chill self. "What do you need help with?"

Still very unsure of what the fuck that exactly was, she thought it best to get down to what she needed him for... "A TV."

"A TV?"

She nodded. "Yes, as big as you can get me."

It didn't take long for Angel to realize it was to piss Drago off. Smiling, he seemed to like where this was going.

Amo, however, wasn't going to catch on till much later.

"Why don't you come with me?" Angel told her. "I can take care of her for the day, Amo. You can go on home."

The big one stared her brother down. "I can't do that. You know I can't."

"We can all go," she assured them, not wanting to start a fight between the two.

The two men didn't disagree as they continued to stare at the other.

Quickly, Kat put down a bowl of water and a can of cat food her brother had dropped off earlier with Shadow before setting down the disposable litter tray he had also brought. Patting Shadow's head, she was ready to leave. "I need to go get a few other things as well."

Angel could only smile bigger.

I'VE LEARNED YOU CAN NEVER BE OVERPREPARED WHEN IT COMES TO THE TIME OF THE MONTH

T*he day was spent productively*, getting the few but necessary things she needed in order to make herself comfortable in *her* new home. Since legally, everything was half hers now—if Drago wanted to play that game.

Angel had gotten her a huge flat screen and set it up. It was now proudly placed on the dresser that they had moved over a bit to sit in front of the couch. It didn't look so great, but she wasn't going for esthetically pleasing at this point. She just wanted a fucking TV. 'Cause what freaking house didn't have a TV, for Christ's sake?

While Angel did that, she had taken the time to settle in, putting away her things and making sure she was obnoxious in the placement of them. *I just can't wait for hubby to get home.*

The dynamic between her brother and Amo hadn't really changed; they just seemed to ignore each other better as the day went on. There was a reason why Angel was wary of him, and she figured she should be too, as her brother was a good judge of character. That was what he was known for.

It wasn't hard to realize Amo clearly hated them. She'd known within the first five minutes that he hated her for her last name, but that wasn't anything new to her or Angel. However, there was something else there that made Amo especially bad to her brother, and she wondered if she was going to have to find out on her own, or if he was going to finally break down and tell her.

Kat found herself keeping her distance from him, wondering exactly how safe she might just be around him when her brother wasn't there, but it wasn't until she turned around from finally putting all her clothes away that she saw Amo had actually set up the things she had gotten for Shadow and was now petting her pretty black cat as he rubbed up against the giant.

Unlike Drago, Amo appeared to like Shadow and have a soft spot for animals, and just like that, the fear she was beginning to build up for Amo quickly disappeared. As tough and as harsh he might be on the outside, she could see what his heart really held, just with a single pet to her cat.

Kat could only smile as she went to go throw in a bag of popcorn, wanting to join her brother on the couch with the movie he just turned on, but she didn't get so lucky when the front door opened and her so-called "hubby" came in.

"What the fuck??"

As quick as he turned on the TV, Angel turned it back off, getting up from the couch. "Look at the time. Adalyn's probably waiting for me."

Drago continued to stand there angrily stunned.

"Remember, I'm just a couple doors down," her brother warned him as he passed to leave, then shut the door.

"Why is there a huge-ass TV in my living room?"

"We're *married* now, remember? So, it's *our* living room," she corrected him.

Ready to blow, he asked a question he might not want to know the answer to. "How big is it?"

She played dumb, watching the microwave with a smile. "I don't know, like fifty?"

"Seventy," Amo corrected, realizing exactly what Kat had reeled him into.

"Why the hell did you let her get one that big?" Drago barked at him coming closer, but then he finally saw it. "What in the hell is this!?"

"A cat tree."

"A tree? You got one the size of a mountain!"

"Shadow needs his exerci—"

"Is that a damn litterbox in my living room!!!!!!"

Kat took the bag out of the microwave. "He can always shit on the floor, if you'd rather that."

"There's a bathroom. Put it in there!" Drago reached down, seeing it was clean before he picked it up, and headed for the bathroom.

Looking over at Amo, she decided to give him a warning. "You might want to leave."

"Why?" Amo asked, but right when he finished the word, he heard Drago's boom again.

"WHAT IN GOD'S—"

Quickly, Amo went to the front door and walked the hell out.

"—NAME IS THIS SHIT!"

She practically danced to the couch, then plopped down to turn on her brand-new seventy-inch flat screen TV.

"Katarina...," Drago spoke her name very calmly yet irate at the same time. "Why did you feel the need to cover *OUR*"—he said that word rather sarcastically before he continued—"bathroom in tampons and pads?"

She shrugged looking through what she should watch. "I've learned you can never be overprepared when it comes to the time of the month."

"If you're not careful, this marriage isn't going to end in divorce...." Drago went to stand in front of the huge TV, so she could hear his next few words very carefully. "It's going to end in murder."

Satisfied she paid him back, she smiled brightly before she kept flicking the channels pretending that he wasn't standing in front of it. When it landed on the perfect TV show, she kept it there as the title screen of *Deadly Women* started to play.

"Witch," he mumbled harshly under his breath, taking the warning before he turned around to grab some clothes out of the drawer.

"Why do you keep calling me that?"

"Let's see... the only color I've seen you in is black. You have a creepy-ass cat. You probably sacrificed someone to be that good at math, and you are currently watching a show where women try to get away with murder."

Well, that was descriptive and mostly true. "So, when you say 'witch,' you don't mean it like 'bitch'?"

"Yeah, sure," he grumbled, clearly on the verge of killing her.

In that context, she could take being called that as a compliment.

By the time the woman on the show killed her husband, Drago had to walk away. When he started to walk upstairs, a giggling Kat couldn't help but curiously watch him walk up, still wondering what exactly was up there.

Instead of going to see what it was, she used the alone time to change into comfier clothes, and by the time she was finished, she heard a knock on the door, her last surprise for Drago coming right on time.

Kat went to the door to open it before he made it to the top of the steps to see who it was. When Maria, followed by Adalyn, Lake, Elle, and Chloe, came in, Drago went right back to whatever the fuck he was doing.

"Brought some pizza," Adalyn happily said, going to the couch looking like she was ready to eat and get the party started.

Lake practically ran with her. "And I got the soda!"

"We brought the movies," Elle said as she and Chloe laid down the options on the coffee table in front of them.

"And I brought my company." Maria plopped down in her pink velvet outfit that shockingly wasn't a dress. "You're welcome."

Joining the girls, Kat thought she could get used to this aspect of being married if it meant she had a group of girls to be around for the first time in her life, as she took herself a slice of pizza. "Thank you all so much. This is awesome."

"You're welcome." Sweet Elle spoke on behalf of all of them while looking through all the chick flicks they had brought. "What should we watch—"

Chloe interrupted her, staring at the TV. "W-What is this?"

"Oh. It's called *Deadly Women*." Kat looked for the remote to change the channel, not sure if the girl could handle it.

Everyone looking at the TV went silent to listen, but it was the tall brunette who cocked her head to the side to ask the question that was going to become obvious in about five seconds. "What's it about?"

Since Drago had put it so eloquently, she used his wording. "It's about women who try getting away with murder."

Finally finding the remote, she was about to change it.

"Wait." Maria stopped her. "This looks interesting."

KAT IN WONDERLAND

"Holy shit!" Adalyn shoved another handful of popcorn down her throat when a woman poisoned her husband who was already dying of cancer.

Elle couldn't look away from the TV. "I don't understand. He was weeks away from dying."

Kat had already seen this episode before, and no one could figure out the reason why she did it, but it was Maria who finally solved the case.

The blonde popped a single kernel in her mouth. "He just wasn't dying fast enough."

Chloe's eyes went wide. Surprising them all, she was entertained by the show as well as they continued their marathon. "Oh my—"

"Jesus," Lake finished for her, but then picked up her phone when it dinged. "Vincent said I have five seconds to get home, or he is gonna come in here to get me."

Collectively, they all looked at their phones to see how late it was.

"Crap." The sweet blonde saw the messages from Nero.

"Yeah, I need to go too," Chloe agreed, seeing hers from Lucca.

"Ha-ha, Angel's the one who said I could stay as long as I want."

Yeah, well, that's 'cause he's probably glad I'm not alone with Drago.

Hurriedly, they cleaned up, then filed out of the apartment. With Maria going last out the door, Kat stopped her before she could leave.

"Can I ask you something?" She kept her voice low for only her to hear.

The tall blonde nodded her head seeing it was serious. "Of course."

It was a risk for her to ask this of his sister, but she had to know the truth. The killer did try to kill her, after all, and she needed to know who she had to stay the fuck away from. "Did Lucca find out about Todd taking you to go wedding dress shopping?"

"Yes." Maria gave her the harsh truth. "But if you are thinking what I think you are thinking, it's not Lucca."

Getting what she needed to know, she gave her a nod pretending to agree with her.

Only time will tell.

Being sure to smile as she left, not wanting to alarm her while she closed the door, she went back to the couch, her mind turning to Drago, who hadn't come back down the steps.

What is he doing up there? Kat picked up the remote and turned down the TV to better hear what he might be doing. When she heard metal clacking every now and then, she wondered if she should go up there but decided against it, not wanting to invade his privacy. He hadn't told her what was up there, and it was probably for a reason.

Getting herself comfortable on the sofa, she had to admit that it was a great day, and it wasn't long before she fell fast asleep…

…It took Kat longer to heal than her brothers, but at least it would be a long time before he came for her again. With her three older brothers taking the hits before her, she received his brutality the least, only getting a hold of her if Dominic wasn't around or wasn't physically able. This last time though, it was the first time he had to watch.

She noticed his presence changed the second she woke up. A silent power radiated through him, which intensified the more she healed. By the time the bruises left her body, Dominic spoke to her differently.

"I didn't come down for that," he told her when she reached for her homework to show him.

She scrunched up her nose. They always worked on school stuff, especially math. "You didn't?"

He shook his head.

Kat put her stuff away, going to sit closer to him on the bed. "What's wrong?" she asked, confused.

"We have to do something," he told her, looking down at her with a serious expression. "You know our little secret?"

She nodded.

"We have to tell him now."

"W-We do?" Now she really didn't understand. Her brother had told her to keep the secret ever since he'd figured it out.

"Yes." Dom held out his hand for her to take it. When she placed hers in his, he looked at her sternly. "You ready?"

This time when she nodded, she had to put on a brave face. Even at ten years old she knew once the secret came out, her life was going to change forever.

Following him up the stairs, she squeezed his hand for dear life when they stood in front of the devil as he sat at the table counting money.

"I thought you knew better than to show me her face," Lucifer spewed to his son with a hateful tongue.

Dominic ignored him, whispering in her ear before he smiled at her. "Go show him what you can do, Kat."

"What the fuck do you thin—"

"Just give her a minute," his son told him.

Trying to be brave like her brother had taught her, she walked closer to the devil.

"Do. Not. Touch. Her." The twenty-year-old warned in a tone that his father would sometimes respect.

Knowing that her brother was here to protect her, she sat down at the table next to Lucifer, then started picking up the scattered money he had yet to count, placing matching bills on top of one another. She was at it for a bit, carefully sorting out all the money till all the stacks were laid out in a row going from ones to hundreds.

"Five thousand three hundred and ninety-seven."

Lucifer, who had just sat there the whole time, watching her work, now looked at his son. "Is she right?"

"Yes," he assured him without a doubt in his mind. "But you can count it, if you want."

"She's special..." The devil leaned forward in his chair, staring at the little girl he'd never wanted to call his daughter right in her eyes. "Like him*."*

"She is," he confirmed. "Do not make the same mistake again by leading her right to our enemies."

Lucifer's dead black eyes snapped back to his son's at the insult. "Is there anything else you want to fucking say?"

"She is too valuable to us." Dominic placed his hands on the table before he stood. Staring the devil down, he showed him the monster he had created. "And you will not touch her again."...

... Kat woke up about an hour later unsure if it was from the memory or from still hearing the clatter of metal that was now accompanied by grunting. Beginning to worry, she got up from the couch having to move a sleeping Shadow to do so before she started walking up the steps. She figured if he really didn't want her up there, he would have told her so. Unsure of what she expected when she reached the top of the steps, she probably should have guessed.

Standing there for several minutes, she had another moment of seeing him for what he was. That was what happened when a person didn't know you were watching, and with Drago it was almost mesmerizing to watch.

He was wearing only gym shorts, his body drenched in sweat from the vigorous workout—she couldn't dream of ever doing—with his legs and his good arm. It was obvious he was trying to get back to the form he once had before, practically killing himself up here for hours to do so, but it was that look in his eyes of pure determination that truly enthralled her.

Like Dominic, Lucifer hadn't marked him like the others. He made him stronger. It was so rare she thought she would only see it in Dominic, but now she could see the same mark in Drago. Both men had an unmatched strength, refusing to let the devil win, even when they might have failed.

Turning around, she headed back down the steps undetected and walked to the fridge to get something before heading back up. This time when she reached the top, she made sure her presence was known.

Drago curiously looked at her while wiping the sweat off his face with the T-shirt he had hanging over his shoulder.

She handed him a protein shake. It was her way of calling a truce.

"Thank you."

Kat took a seat on the bench beside him, feeling a bit guilty. "I'm sorry if I pushed you too far. In hindsight, since we're married now and all, I should have told you about the stuff I wanted, and I probably shouldn't have gotten the most obnoxious, biggest size there was."

It was the first genuine laugh she heard from him. "Probably."

"I can return them and get a *normal* size TV and cat tree." She laughed with him.

"Keep 'em. Like you said, Shadow needs his exercise, and by the sounds of it, I think the girls would be pretty upset if I let you return the TV. I wouldn't put it past Maria to kill me for that."

Kat laughed louder, not at the joke, but at how accurate his statement probably was.

"You know, the only reason I didn't have a TV was because I didn't have anyone to watch it with."

Ow. Was her heart starting to hurt?

"I probably should have gotten one before you got here, but if I had known you wanted one so bad, I would have bought you one, Kat."

Yep. It was everything she could do not to grab her chest at this point. "Thanks, I'll keep that in mind from now on."

"Good." Drago opened the bottle and started to suck down the much-needed liquid. "Who bought all that stuff for you?"

"Angel." She laughed once more, feeling bad for her poor brother she'd used to get back at Drago.

"All right." He nodded, drinking the last drop.

"I don't think you should be working out like this considering you have stitches from a bullet you took just a day ago."

"I've worked myself harder with less," he assured her, showing his determination yet again even if it did make him look crazy.

"Well, you're not going to keep working out, are you?"

Seeing that she was worried, he assured her once more, "No, I'm done."

"Good." She breathed a sigh of relief. It was obvious he was exhausted, whether he admitted it or not. She took another look at the room past all the weights, taking notice of something. "Is this supposed to be a gym?"

"No. It's technically supposed to be the bedroom. Those doors lead to a bathroom and closet."

"Really?" Curiously, she stood and went to a door that opened up into a huge walk-in closet that held some suits before she opened the other door that went into the most amazing bathroom that had two sinks, a walk-in shower with two rainfall spouts, and a beautiful soaking tub. The one downstairs was a miniature version if this one, with only a sink and a shower. "This was up here the whole time, and you didn't tell me?! Why haven't you been using this?"

When she came back out, it looked like Drago was about to say something, but then he closed his mouth before finally answering, "I suppose we should move up here now, huh?"

"I mean, only if you want. . . ." Her voice trailed off. For some reason, she felt guilty changing a man she'd only been married to for a day.

"Yeah, it'll be cool to properly use this space." Getting up, he actually gave her a smile. "I'll try and find time to work on doing that for you."

"Thank you." She found herself smiling back wondering what kind of rabbit hole she'd fallen in when she'd walked up those steps. With both of them going back downstairs, she only hoped… she didn't find her way back out.

Kat in Wonderland had a nice ring to it. Don't you think?

It just might.

THE FUCKING RABBIT HOLE

Drago came down the steps starving, then ate all the leftover pizza before he took a quick shower.

She, however, went back to her couch still exhausted from her long day, but by the time he finally went to bed, she couldn't get herself as comfortable on this godforsaken couch as she had earlier.

"Christ." When she did her tenth roll to try to get comfy, Drago couldn't stand to hear her toss and turn any longer. "I'm not sleeping naked, Katarina, and I'll even put a pillow between us if it makes you happy, if you would just sleep on the damn bed."

Kat thought about it for a moment, unsure if she should.

"I only touch women who want to be touched, Katarina, even if that woman is my wife." He gave her a promise before he leaned up and slammed a pillow down beside him to get her to feel comfortable enough to join him. "Now, get the hell over here."

"Fine!" she finally agreed, getting up and climbing into the empty side of the bed.

The little bell around Shadow's neck got louder as he jumped up in bed, then sat on the pillow wedged between them, using it as his own personal bed.

"Hell no, I said *you* could sleep up here," Drago hissed before he looked at the cat, realizing exactly why Kat might have called her cat Shadow. "Not *you*."

Kat gave Shadow a nice pet. "Try and move him, then."

He stared into the eyes that glowed yellow in the night which were now sinisterly staring him down like he understood every word they'd spoken. Drago's mind seemed to quickly change when he rolled over and pulled the blankets up around him like they were a barrier.

She was grateful he couldn't see the smile that now tilted her lips in the dark.

With the purring in her ear, it wasn't going to take long for her to drift to sleep in a sea filled with dreams. Just as she was nodding off, she heard his voice, which seemed to hold a bit of guilt of his own.

"I didn't want to ever get married either… I just wanted you to know that."

Kat could have taken it as an insult, like she had meant it when she'd thrown those hateful words at him earlier, but she didn't. Instead, she knew all too well what he meant.

This time when she would drift off to sea, it wouldn't be just her; it would be both of them, as they sat in the same boat. Together.

Waking up the next day felt very different for her. Strangely, she couldn't stop smiling as she took her shower, and by the time she put on her oversized Metallica shirt, black skinny jeans, and she exited the bathroom, she realized it might have felt very different for the both of them—on account of the overwhelming aroma of eggs and bacon.

Turning the corner, she found a fully-suited Drago taking the eggs out of the pan.

"That's a lot of—" She took in the excessive amount, putting only two eggs and two strips of bacon on a plate that was laid out. "Meat. How is all this going to get eate—"

Amo came through the door as if he followed a scented trail. Taking a plate, he began stacking a massive amount on it. Then Drago took the healthy amount of food that was left, then they all took a seat at the kitchen island.

She knew body builders needed to eat a lot of food, but *DAMN.*

"I mostly just have protein shakes, so Amo can take you to the grocery store today if you would like, to get you whatever you want."

Kat nodded as she watched the two put away the meat-filled plates like they were in sync and almost starved to death.

Downing a glass of water, Drago checked his watch before getting up to put his plate in the sink. Then he came to Katarina and stood beside her.

When she looked up at him from the stool she sat on, her heart might've skipped a beat. Or two.

He reached down into his pocket, retrieving his leather billfold and opening it. "You can keep this till I can get you your own, after I add you to my bank account."

Amo dropped his silver fork out of his hand so suddenly it almost broke the plate underneath, judging from the loud clack.

Staring down at the black card that had the name *Drago De Santis* on it, she almost choked.

"From now on, when you want something, you don't have to ask anyone for it. Not even me."

Did he just— Did he— Kat had to actually grab her chest at the complete loss of words, wondering if she had heard him correctly. The fucking rabbit hole she'd fallen into was starting to get confus—

The lips that took hers weren't hard this time. They were soft. Sweet. Kind. And most of all, tender.

"Don't wait up for me, sweetheart," he told her just like yesterday, before he left her in mostly the same way. Speechless. Except this time, she didn't feel the rage. It was worse and the beginning of…

Oh God.

What is that?

Don't say it. Don't say it. Don't say it.

Love.

IT'S GETTING REALLY WEIRD DOWN HERE

K***at tapped her fingers in*** a rolling motion, staring down at the black credit card while she replayed the last few minutes over and over again in her head. *It's getting really weird down here.*

The way he was acting toward her was... *kinda sweet.* Even though she was being the biggest witch there was since they had gotten married. Which was now really, really making her feel guilty. *I mean, he just trusted a Luciano with his bank card, for Christ's sake.*

It certainly was becoming a new world, and Amo, who had stopped eating seeming to lose his appetite, was seeing it too.

Getting up, he took the rest of his uneaten food to the trash. The shock on his face and his reaction at what unfolded pretty much said it all about how he still felt for the Lucianos, but she tried to not let it bug her.

She didn't know if it hit all married couples, but suddenly, she felt this urge... *to make him happy? Oh God, what is wrong with me?*

She took a breath still staring at the card, wondering if the thought of making him happy was a good idea. She supposed the guilt of being such a witch yesterday caught up to her, when she took out her new cell phone with her new contacts and made a call, but the person she needed help from now was different.

After she hung up the phone, it was not even five seconds before someone barged right through the door.

The beautiful blond Maria came in with an evil yet ecstatic look in her eyes. "So, how can I help piss off Drago today?"

Amo looked like he was about to scream and put his foot down, but Kat had other plans for once.

"Actually, I want to do something nice for him."

"Ugh." Crossing her arms over her chest, Maria didn't seem as thrilled anymore. She mumbled under her breath something only she could hear. "You girls are so weak when it comes to men."

"What?" she asked, not having heard a word she'd said.

"I said, it's going to be a lot less fun for me now, but... how can I help?"

Kat smiled at her. Maria was like a fairy fucking goddess mother who always rode in to save the day.

"I thought maybe you could help me decorate just a little? And we could move the bed upstairs and his weight stuff down here. He said that he would do it, but he seems to have enough on his plate already." She shrugged. Hearing it out loud, it didn't sound so great. "I don't know. I thought it might be a nice surprise for him."

"It is nice." Maria tapped her heel, clearly thinking as her eyes moved around the bare space. "I'm just actually not the right one for the job."

"Really?" With the level of taste Maria had, Kat was shocked to hear her say those words.

"Fashion and home décor are two separate things, Katarina."

At the blonde's scoff, Kat realized that might've been a stupid question. "Okay. Then… who is?"

THE OG

S*eeing sweet Elle followed by* Nero come through the door, she should have guessed it. Of course the strawberry blonde could decorate and make this place a home.

However, when Elle stood back and Nero came in and took a longing look at the walls with his gorgeous emerald eyes, it hadn't dawned on her just yet. "I'm thinking everything needs to go."

"I agree," Maria concurred.

"Excuse me, what? You?"—she stared at the tall, dark, and handsome man, "she called, you?"

Elle couldn't help but giggle.

"Yeah." His green eyes glowed at her. "What's that supposed to mean?"

"Nothing. I just… wasn't expecting that, is all." Kat smiled at him still not exactly understanding how the fuck Nero was whom Maria called.

"Like I said," he began again, "everything goes, except for the TV." He walked through the space, laying out everything that he seemed to envision in his head. "I'm thinking a huge oversized sectional to hold ten or so people in front of the TV. We need a six-chair dining table that can go there, and upstairs you definitely need a king size bed and updated bedroom furniture. That should get us started."

"Okay, that sounds great and all, but uh…" Kat suddenly felt a bit light-headed. "I was thinking simpler, like move his weights downstairs and move the bed upstairs."

"Absolutely not. His gym upstairs has to go. He can go back to using the hotel gym like the rest of us."

She stopped him right fucking there. "Oh no-no-no-no-no. I think you've really misunderstood. I'm trying to do something nice for Drag—"

Nero shut her up with just a look. "I understand. That's why we're doing what I said."

To say she was nervous at the can of worms she just might've opened was an understatement. That handsome yet somewhat scary man was going to get her killed when her husband came back to find his gym missing.

"Kat, really." He looked at her confused as to why she was freaking out about it. "The bed used to be upstairs until we moved it, and he likes the hotel gym. As far as the furniture, he won't miss it. It's all old and cheap."

"Wait, what? You moved it?" she asked, confused herself now.

"Yeah. When Drago woke up from the coma, we moved his bed and dresser down here because we weren't sure if he was going to be able to walk upstairs again. Then, when he did, he moved some old gym equipment we had upstairs because I don't think he wanted to go to the hotel gym till he got his strength back. But he's okay now. This will all make him happy, trust me." Nero gave her an assuring look.

That information she was just given hurt like fucking hell. He hadn't told her that when he could have last night, so she felt like she knew a secret about him that she shouldn't have. It was also hard to take considering it was her father who'd turned his life upside down. The words, *we weren't sure if he was going to be able to walk upstairs again,* couldn't help but make her feel somewhat responsible, considering her father was no longer alive to take the blame.

"Nero's right. He'll love it," his sister agreed.

It was everything she could do to hold herself together at the moment. She steadied her voice, the guilt inside of her only ratchetting up higher, but by the eager look in his emerald eyes, she could only hope this whole thing didn't backfire. "All right."

Nero rubbed his hands together with a gorgeous sly smile on his face, making himself look like the OG that he was. "Let's do this."

The strawberry blonde was practically ready to swoon.

Damn. Your first true love really was the finest.

When Angel opened the door to his apartment, one of his brows drew up.

"This should be enough for what you got Katarina yesterday." Drago handed him a stack full of cash.

Shaking his head, Angel didn't want to take the money. "I don't—"

"Take it," he demanded harshly. "I want you to know that Katarina will be taken care of. She is my responsibility now, and..." His harsh tone seemed to dissipate into a sincere one. "I want not only you but *all* her brothers to know that."

Angel stared at him for a moment, seeing that he meant every word before he finally took the money. Showing that he respected what he had to say, it was a truce.

Turning away, Drago couldn't believe that he had actually just done that.

Okay, fuck. He liked the little witch when she was nice and… a smartass. You know why? 'Cause she was his little witch now. Even if he didn't want a wife. But like Lucca had said, he'd chosen her, and boy was it turning out that he had chosen her for a reason.

"You're about fifty short," Angel yelled at him as he walked down the hallway.

He didn't even turn around when he yelled back at him, "Well, then you shouldn't have let her get that fucking mountain of a cat tree."

THE MONSTER THAT LAY JUST BENEATH THE SURFACE

To *say her surprise got* blown out of proportion would be an understatement. Nero had gone to an upscale furniture store, practically buying everything on the floor, and somehow came out with a ten-percent discount. Then he brought in every Caruso he could get his hands on to help unload it and get it in the apartment. While the furniture moved in, Elle, Adalyn, and Lake helped her put all their clothes in the walk-in closet, with Maria giving them directions of how to properly do so.

By the time Nero got everything staged, it looked magazine ready.

"Whoa." She felt butterflies rise her stomach, nervous for when Drago would get home. It looked amazing but also so amazing that she was wondering if she should have had him involved. "Thank you all so much."

"I think it's so sweet you did this," Elle told her. "Usually, the men surprise us, but it's so awesome a girl could finally do it."

"About time," Maria mumbled under her breath.

"Yes, it's so much sweeter." Adalyn was smiling ear to ear.

Vincent seemed to get offended. "Why is it sweeter when she does it than when I did it?"

"Thank God, you're pretty." The words fell out of her mouth before she could stop them.

Lake laughed while she took her boyfriend's hand. "Let's go before you embarrass yourself more."

The pretty boy smiled at Kat while his girlfriend and sister had to drag him to the door to leave, seeming to completely miss the insult part of her statement. "She said I was pretty."

Maria rolled her eyes, following them out. "Yeah, but she also thinks you're a dumbass."

"Good luck." Elle gave her a wink.

"Nero—" She looked at the green eyes not knowing where to start or what to even think of him anymore. When they had gone furniture shopping, there was no way in hell she was going to spend Drago's money like that on the day he gave her the card, but Nero had assured her not to worry and that it was a wedding gift from the Carusos. "Thank you for everything. I don't know how to repay you."

"We're family," Nero said in an instant, putting it so simply. "You don't have to."

It was the fucking nicest thing anyone had ever said to her, and if Elle weren't so Goddamn sweet and perfect, she'd almost think Elle was the lucky one.

With everyone besides Amo gone now, it somehow all worked out perfectly as Drago hadn't returned home yet even though it was well into the night. There was only one last thing she needed to go and get.

"I'm going to go to Chloe's. Do you need to come with me?" she asked, opening the door, unsure if Amo needed to watch her with her just going down the hall.

He seemed to get nervous for a second before he answered, "No. I can watch you from here."

"Okay." She found it a bit odd when he just stood outside the apartment door and watched her walk to Chloe's apartment. Knocking on the door, she shouldn't have been surprised when Lucca answered, but it was always a shock when her eyes landed on that frightening man.

Unlike when she came to their apartment earlier, Lucca let her come in this time.

Walking into the gorgeous space was almost unreal. Getting the corner apartment meant two full walls of windows to look down on the city, and with how natural everything was in there, it felt as if you were outside.

"H-Hi." Chloe smiled at her from the couch while Shadow laid on her lap.

"Hey." Kat couldn't help but smile back, going to the couch to sit carefully next to them with some distance in between.

"I'm going to go take a shower." The dangerous man looked at the broken girl, making sure she was okay before he left the room.

"Thanks for watching him for me. I was afraid he would get out with everyone going in and out."

Chloe just kept petting his silky black fur. "You're welcome. I loved having Shadow around."

"He likes you." She watched the two for a moment, listening to Shadow's purr and the way he was with her. "You know, Shadow's very special."

"How?" she asked, raising a scarred brow.

Some animals were blessed with a gift, and Shadow was one of them. She'd often found Shadow cuddled up next to Matthias, as a way to "heal" her brother. The closer he became to a human, she recognized the higher level of pain that person had. Unsure of how to word it, she tried the best she could. "He likes to take a person's pain away."

"Oh."

Kat didn't want to upset her, but she also felt an undying need for the girl not to feel alone. Swallowing hard, she whispered what she'd never talked about, "He hurt me too."

Chloe's gray eyes looked into the black ones that were reminiscent of her demon's, but she could see the pain that she, too, held. Biting her lip, the girl slowly extended a pale, shaky hand.

When she took her hand and gave it a squeeze, Katarina's heart almost broke in two. She knew what it meant that Chloe allowed her to touch her even for a moment. It was somewhat painful to sit so close to the girl after knowing what her father had done to her. Lucifer was a monster, but what she couldn't understand was why she was living with another.

Kat nervously looked back to where Lucca had gone and heard the shower running. What she was about to say could very well get her killed, but she couldn't be who she was if she didn't say anything. "I'm not sure why you're with Lucca, but he is a powerful man. . . ." Taking a breath, she continued giving a hint as to what she was talking about without saying it outright. "Like my father was."

The pale, beautiful, scarred face stared at her for a second before she nodded, understanding what she meant.

Kat could see the girl had an idea about Lucca, but she wasn't sure if she had truly seen the monster that lay just beneath the surface. However, it wasn't her life, and the girl wasn't blind. Kat had seen it instantly in Lucca, and she hoped Chloe would see it too one day. She needed to say one last thing. "You just deserve better."

When she heard the shower turn off, she almost didn't want to take Shadow from the scarred beauty when she picked him up off her lap. "You know, you can come over anytime to see him."

"Thank you." Chloe smiled, happy to hear her offer.

Going for the door, she wanted to get out before the monster returned, but before she could, she heard Chloe's voice, stopping her in her tracks. What she heard the girl say, she wouldn't have expected in a million years.

"Lucca tells me I don't deserve him either."

THE FUCKING POINT OF HAVING A HUSBAND

"What are you doing?" Drago asked when the elevator doors opened as she passed with Shadow in her hands.

Her stomach sank, becoming nervous. "Uhh."

Seeing Amo coming down the hallway, she saw his body tense further. What's going on?"

Usually words came easily to Katarina, but nothing seemed to fall out of her mouth.

Amo was no help when he left the two alone.

"Kat… what did you do?" he asked sternly, obviously sensing she had done something yet again.

Oh God. Please don't let this go bad.

"Don't hate me," she said before she opened the door to the

apartment, letting Shadow down when she did.

Drago slowly walked into the apartment. Very quietly, he looked around, seeing all the new furniture that filled up his space. His once bachelor pad had finally turned into… a home.

The longer he went without saying anything, the sicker she felt. Horrible words never hurt when you were a witch and the one to say hateful things to a person in the first place. But when you did something nice to make someone happy, and they didn't appreciate it, it hurt. Like hell.

Preparing herself for the worst, she braced herself.

"I don't know what to say…" Drago seemed to be speechless, his voice going slightly hoarse. "This is amazing, Kat."

"You like it?!"

"Of course, why wouldn't I?" Clearly he didn't understand why she was so surprised that he did. Looking around, he kept finding new things. "How did you get all this done?"

"I had loooots of help. And Nero," she added.

"I should have known." Drago's smile was momentary before it disappeared. "What happened to your cat tree?"

"Well…" She looked at the much smaller but reasonably-sized cat tree. "Nero made me return it and said I could have one that didn't take up half the apartment."

"I think that was a good choice."

Kat giggled. "Me too."

"Do I get to look upstairs now?" There was an excited glow in his eyes at seeing the transformation.

"Y-Yeah." She grew nervous yet again as she went up the stairs behind him, hoping he wouldn't hate her for letting Nero get rid of his gym.

No words came out of Drago upon seeing their new bedroom filled with updated furniture.

She grew impatient for him to answer. "If you don't like it, we can put it ba—"

"Kat, come here." He demanded her to come closer to where he stood. When she slowly approached, he took her face in his hands. "Why did you think I wouldn't like it?"

It was hard for her to put her thoughts together as she was staring up at him so closely. "Nero said that you wouldn't mind, but I should have asked you if it would be oka—"

"I love it." Drago leaned down, his lips brushing the side of her cheek. "Thank you."

Kat stiffened, self-consciously remaining still. If she looked at him, they would be kissing, and she didn't know if Drago wanted to kiss her, or if she was the only one who wanted to kiss until their lips were sore. Equal parts of dread and excitement battled inside of her knowing that the second their lips met, they might not stop.

Drago was fucking attractive, and she wouldn't be the first woman who wondered how he would kiss when he really meant it, and if he was even capable of being gentle while doing so. Gentleness wasn't what came to a woman's mind, when looking at the Caruso bodyguard.

A firm hand on her chin took the choice out of her hands as her face was turned. A hairsbreadth separated their lips. She desperately wanted to lick her suddenly dry ones but was terrified that Drago would misinterpret the movement.

Using his free hand, he picked up a pretty pink strand of silky hair. "You're not nervous, are you, Kitty Kat?"

She couldn't take it any longer. She had to lick her lips. She just wished she hadn't stared so intently at his juicy-looking ones as she did. "No."

He came just an inch closer, so his chest pressed against her breasts.

Katarina suddenly felt surrounded by the warmth of his body. He hadn't removed his hand from her chin, and she felt imprisoned in his grip even though a small voice in the back of her mind told her it was safe to pull away. It was those hell-bent eyes that held her spellbound.

He leaned closer and finally slid his lips over hers so softly she couldn't be sure that he actually had. It was only when she felt the glide of his tongue on the seam of her tightly closed mouth that she realized she wasn't imagining it.

"Kiss me, Katarina."

Oh fuck. She shivered at the temptation, unconsciously parting her lips to let Drago's tongue slip inside her mouth. Their breaths mingling was just as erotic as giving in to Drago's exploring mouth, becoming embarrassed at the small moan that escaped her.

Drago had kissing down to an art. He wasn't an inexperienced boy; no, Drago was anything but inexperienced. The man who had her heart beating out of her chest and her hands gripping his shoulders to pull him closer wasn't a novice. Drago knew exactly what he was doing, which was sending off darts of need to her sensitive body parts that she had never paid attention to before.

Shifting, she thought at first that he was pulling away but found herself lifted upward and taken to their new bed. Sitting on his lap as a seeking hand went to her thigh, she made no attempt to move it, clutching his shoulders tighter.

Drago's arms went around her ribcage, tugging her tighter against him. "Should I stop?"

She buried her face in the crook of his neck, knowing when she finally let him get their first deep kiss, there was going to be no stopping.

"No," she mumbled.

When his mouth returned to hers once more, Kat was the one to let her tongue slip into his, wanting to taste all that he had to give as her fingers went to his hair to feel the smooth texture. She gripped his hair harder when one of his hands went to her thighs, gradually sliding intimately between her legs.

Her muscles tensed as his hand slid back up to cup her mound just beneath her jeans, sending trembling sensations storming through her body. It was like being hungry and not knowing what you wanted to satisfy the craving that was slowly leading her searching down a tunnel that she didn't know where it was leading.

Kat only knew she wanted to come out the other end in one piece. As Drago unsnapped her jeans, she quickly began to doubt that was going to happen. Each touch of his fingertips led a trail of fire along her skin that matched his eyes. When his fingers finally touched the soft, moist flesh between her thighs, she was consumed by the scorching heat. It all centered on the throbbing nub that

Drago tantalized by barely skimming the aching point of her desire.

She gave a startled scream when his thumb pressed down before swirling downward to find her opening.

When a large finger entered her to his knuckle, her back arched at the sensation. She felt herself being shifted until she was flat on her back and Drago was above her. She knew he wasn't going to ask her if she wanted him to stop again; that point had passed for them both. Unabashedly, one of her thighs fell to the side, opening herself even more to his touch before her hips lurched awkwardly under his hand trying to drive his finger deeper within her. The hunger inside of her wanted more, but she didn't know how to get it or how to make Drago put the fire out that was stealing every thought from her head.

Not releasing her just yet, he removed his finger only to slide two back in, making it a tight fit within her.

A whimper escaped at the burning sensation he had just given her. He carefully cooled it down as his thick fingers coaxed her insides, and it wasn't long before she wanted even more. Much, much more than what he was doing to her now.

Kat wasn't going to ask but beg for what she wanted next, but the second her mouth opened to do so, his thumb rolled over her clit in a way that had her crying out in pleasure.

Placing a light kiss on her stunned lips, he removed his fingers that were still deep in her.

Did I just—

He placed another light kiss on her rosy cheek as he buttoned her jeans back up.

Is he just— Her body was only just beginning to feel the need fulfilled. "That's it?" The words fell out of her mouth, her foggy brain feeling frustrated.

"Yes." Drago smiled down at her. "For now."

Kat wasn't holding on to her virginity for any special reason; it was simply that there had been no one to give it to. Being one of the unlucky ones, she'd never built up her virginity as something to be protected or cherished, too afraid that it would be stolen from her, giving her another scar for life.

She wanted sex to be what it was meant to be, for pleasure, not to be used as a form of abuse or to feel pain. She wanted to have control over her body, and with Drago, she felt she did. She felt a sudden need he could give fulfilled; she felt in control as though she could ask him to stop at any time, and he would. But most importantly, Drago could take away the fear of her possibly losing her virginity to someone to whom it didn't belong.

It should have been a win-win, but watching him get up off the bed and leave her without doing exactly that frustrated her. She had seen the fire in his eyes, seen that he didn't want to leave her there without taking more, so why didn't he?

I mean, what's the fucking point of having a husband if they can't—

Fuck.

Drago had lain in bed for over an hour just staring at the pink hair that seemed to glow in the moonlight while she slept. He had let himself touch her, something he hadn't wanted to allow himself to do just yet. He'd found himself swept up in the moment from the sweet act she had done for him, and lost control of himself by losing himself in her.

Thankfully, he stopped himself before it went further. Only the guilt he would feel of defiling her had stopped him. Even though they were married, she was much younger than him and didn't belong to him just because he'd picked her out of a line.

If or *when* he would allow himself to take her, it would have to be a cold day in hell. For that guilt of possibly ruining her life to die inside of him, all because Katarina was the only one who could give him the revenge he so desperately desired.

He had won. There was no denying it. Drago had taken what had mattered most to the Luciano men, their sister. The price they paid was far greater than those five bullets and three months he'd spent in purgatory.

For him, it turned out revenge wasn't that sweet. And now, every time he looked at his wife since saying "I do," he was only reminded of how he had used her and ruined the rest of her life. It only hurt worse the more time he spent with her, to find that the cost the Luciano brothers had to pay was priceless. That was why he didn't have it in himself to be mean or hurtful to her any longer, because he had to wake up every fucking day and look at himself in the mirror.

Lucifer might have killed him, but it was Drago who'd created the monster.

FACE-TO-FACE

T*he remaining night after what* they had shared was calm yet empty, but waking up the next day to realize Drago had left in the early morning made her feel emptier.

She had dressed and come down the steps to find the dreaded Amo sitting on the couch, but it wasn't long after her feet left the stairs and stepped onto the floor that her heart sank to meet them.

THUD.

The door being kicked quick and hard into the apartment had Katarina jolting around. When her eyes fell on the dangerous man at the door, she shouldn't have been shocked to find Amo hadn't moved an inch.

The demonic man stalked into the room, carefully creeping up to her like she was his prey.

Sure of death to come, she stood there strong and ready to face her killer.

"Katarina...."

Her skin turned as cold as his voice. Swallowing hard, she knew well enough that her time had come.

"Why don't you ask Amo what happens when you jeopardize my relationship with Chloe?" His voice cut colder this time.

Now, Amo had finally moved, standing up from the couch where he'd lazily sat, his uncaring demeanor quickly changing into confusion over what was happening.

She was just as confused, looking to Amo before her eyes turned back to the boogieman.

"Amo is not allowed to see her, speak to her, or be in her presence ever again because he thought *his* love for her and hatred of *me* could come between us." It was Lucca who glanced at him, this time with disdain in his eyes. "And now here he stands, only alive because I wouldn't be able to look at her beautiful face if I killed him."

Those cold bones in her body started to lightly shake.

"Leave us," he demanded of Amo.

However, Amo didn't move. A protective expression finally covered his face.

She knew the boogieman would only give one final warning. "Leave. *Now.*"

"I-It's okay," Kat managed to say, assuring him in hopes that she would be all right.

Amo walked slowly and what seemed to be regretfully as he left the apartment, closing the door behind him and leaving Kat to face her demon.

"I think you have mistaken my kindness as weakness, Katarina." Lucca reached out, grabbing her chin with a light force like he had the first time they'd met. "Or been mistaken that I had any kindness at all."

"You're the one mistaken…," she whispered on a shudder, already knowing there was no kindness in him. And finally, the truth would come out as it took everything she had to say these next words, "You remind me of my father. I see him in you, and that is why I believe you are the killer."

His eyebrows slightly drew together. "You think I'm One-Shot?"

"Yes," she proclaimed after hearing what she assumed was the killer's nickname.

The cold rage seemed to dissipate into curiosity as he lessened his hold on her chin. "Why?"

"Because Todd disobeyed you, and Chloe wasn't at the wedding. It doesn't seem like coincidence to me."

His grip tightened once more. "When I kill one of my incapable soldiers, it isn't with a bullet, Katarina."

She could see the wickedness in his eyes that showed her exactly why he reminded her of her father and why she thought they were one and the same. However, she could also see the truth in them, having no need to lie to her alone in this room. "And Chloe?" She couldn't help but ask.

"If Chloe went, then Amo couldn't, and I wanted him to go to the wedding and be forced to watch his uncle marry a Luciano." Seeing the now confused look on her face, he continued, "As punishment for nearly breaking every bone in Angel's body."

She licked her dry lips. "Oh."

"You don't seem surprised," Lucca stated, lifting up her chin higher to read her face.

"Angel… already told me."

Smiling, Lucca let her chin go. "Amo doesn't know you know, does he?"

"No."

There was a sort of wonderment as he continued to look down at her. "And Drago?"

"No," she revealed, keeping that secret she had known the day after she'd met Amo. Angel had finally told her, wanting her to know, so she could be wary of him, but remembering the way he was with Shadow, she knew the truth. "He's not evil," And like her brother Matthias, he was… "just broken."

And now I know why.

There was an essence in Lucca that was "all knowing" like he could read minds or see the future. It was an intuitive ability beyond his years that should have been unknown to man, but here he was, living proof that such existed. "Amo will heal when he's ready, but others will never get the chance. You can fix a break, but you can't fix obliteration."

A single tear welled up in her eye before it fell splashing to her cheek, knowing his words to be true for those who walked this earth with a similar pain that Matthias held. The saddest part was they would often hide that pain behind laughter or charisma, but eventually that darkness would overtake them, consuming them for all they were worth till they couldn't take it anymore...

"Do not cry, Katarina, for we need men like him to balance out men like your father..." Reaching out, he wiped the tear with a cold finger. "Me..." Then he rubbed the salty liquid between his fingers before he gave her another all-knowing look. "... and Cassius."

Her heart sunk instantly back to the floor. "How did y—"

"You can't hide pure evil. Even in the form of a boy." The boogieman returned in a flash, showing her that same evil. "I hope we have reached an understanding, Katarina. I like you but not enough that I won't kill you if you speak to Chloe that way again."

It had been a long time since she'd prayed. Watching the boogieman leave after she nodded, she prayed not only for the souls he had taken, but also that they had been worth sacrificing.

Amo stood on the other side of the door very quietly, listening to every word they were saying.

She knew... this whole time.

Wanting to feel anything but nothing since Chloe, he had chosen hatred. Hatred toward a family that had tried to take his uncle away. A family born from the devil, who he thought there wasn't a one worth saving.

But it turned out… *there's one.*

Drago opened his apartment door to see Katarina asleep on the couch.

Getting up from the table, Amo came up to him face-to-face. "I need to speak with you."

"Okay." He matched his nephew's quiet tone, so they wouldn't wake her up.

"I did something, Drago, that you might not forgive me for."

He paused for a moment as every muscle in his body tensed, worried for what was about to pass through his nephew's lips. Whatever it was, was bad. That he knew in his gut.

"I wanted to get even with the Lucianos after what they did to you, and when I heard Tom died, I think a part of me lost it. So, I set out to even the score."

"What the fuck did you do?" Drago took a grave step toward him.

"While you were gone, I took it out on the Luciano who was closest at the time." His voice didn't waiver, and he didn't sugarcoat it as he stood there strongly, confessing his sin. "Angel."

"You were one of them wearing the mask." It wasn't a question but a statement, having heard what had happened to Angel when he'd returned to this plane. Lucca had said he was handling it, and with him being so busy recovering, he hadn't thought of it. Truthfully, he hadn't much cared about the Luciano brother being hurt when he first heard it. It was that the Carusos had defied orders, knowing that

Angel was here under Lucca's protection, and committed the crime knowing that it was so severe they needed to hide their faces. "Does Lucca know?"

"I was assigned to watch her"—he nodded to Katarina still peacefully sleeping—"as punishment."

Lucca was a smart man, that was for sure. Forcing him to watch the sister of the one he'd almost killed was serendipitous in a way. Being constantly reminded of the thing you did wrong was a hard pill to swallow, especially when that pill came in the form of Katarina. That he knew all too well. You couldn't hate her, no matter how hard you tried, and Lucca fucking knew that.

He took another step toward him, until his face was an inch away while not only his eyes breathed fire, but his mouth did too. "De Santis men don't like to lose, but you lost *her* to *him*. Now... you are losing yourself."

Amo could only nod.

He stepped away before opening the door. "Get your shit together and get the fuck out of my face."

Closing that door on his nephew was hard, but closing that door on a soldier was easy.

ONE DAY

Hearing the door close, Kat woke up to find Drago was finally home. She dreaded this moment of having to tell him about what she had said to Chloe. She didn't regret saying the words, and that was exactly why she needed to tell him. Wanting to be upfront and honest about how she felt about Lucca, seeing that Drago saw the boogieman differently than she did. It wasn't the bond she wanted to break between the two; she just wanted him to know she saw Lucca no differently than she saw her father.

"Drago I—"

"Oh good." He came over to the couch. "You're awake."

Taking a breath, she needed to go ahead and get it off her chest. "Yeah I—"

"I have a surprise for you, Kat." He smiled as he held out a hand for her to take.

Huh? She was confused but decided to take his hand, letting him lead her to the new dining room table.

He made her sit in front of a thick folder he had placed at the head of the table.

Staring down at the blank folder filled with papers, she grew even more confused, till she flipped it open revealing a bunch of numbers.

"Lucca has asked me to offer you the job of being the Carusos' bookkeeper." He took the empty seat beside her to look in her eyes. "And if you want to accept, then you will have your own office down the hall."

Blinking for a minute straight, she didn't know what to say at first, knowing the importance of the offer she was just given. Women were not given jobs in the mafia, especially when it involved their money. She stared down at the first page, seeing big numbers. "A-Are we talking on or off the books?"

"Whatever you are comfortable with," he told her, not wanting to put any pressure on her. "You can strictly do the books that are legal, if you want."

"Are you serious?" Kat asked, disbelieving of the words she was still hearing. She was a fucking Luciano, for Christ's sake, and what she was staring at right now could bring the entire Caruso family down.

He nodded, in this moment looking at her as if she were a soldier. "Yes."

They might not know what you're capable of, but one day they will. The words had spoken to her before he'd walked her down the aisle echoed in her head.

Well, I'll be damned.

Kat licked her dry lips. "Drago?"

"Yeah?" He sounded as if he expected to hear her accept or decline the offer, honestly anything but what she was about to say next.

"I need you…"—she could only hope that she wasn't about to make another mistake—"to take me to Lucca."

Asking to speak with him alone, she was unaccompanied as she crossed the threshold into Lucca's office. One thing was for sure; it was much different standing in front of the boogieman when you were the one to seek him out.

She didn't know how she'd pictured meeting with him, but seeing him behind the big wooden desk made it that much more daunting. Taking the seat in front of him, she watched him flip a silver lighter, turning it on and off as he curiously stared at her and waited for what she had to say.

"I told Chloe that you were powerful like my father." Kat stared into those cold blue-green eyes finally seeing something different in them. "But the truth is, you are much more powerful than he ever was."

The flame was left steady this time as he let it burn the end of a cigarette he had placed in his mouth. That flame illuminated his face with an orange glow, making him much more attractive than she had seen him before.

"My father kept me hidden in a basement for seventeen years, only letting me come out when he needed his money counted. My brothers were the only ones allowed to know I did that, because Lucifer would rather slit his own daughter's throat than let anyone in the family know that I touched their money before he could disperse it."

Smoke slowly trailed in and out of his mouth as he sat there listening to her.

"I was wrong about you, Lucca Caruso, but you were wrong about yourself too." Kat's lip turned up in one corner. "Deep, deep, deep down, there is a kindness in you that you only show people you respect. It is not lightly given, only to those who you feel can withstand what may come. Only to those who can serve a purpose for you down the road," she told him, seeming to know exactly what he was preparing for. "But unlike my father, you give your respect not only to a man but to a woman."

Hearing every word she spoke, he stared at her, mesmerized like he was for that moment in the apartment earlier.

"I will work for you, Lucca, but you must know one thing. The road you are going down will lead to my brother one day, and I *will* stand by Dominic's side."

A smile touched his lips before he nodded in understanding.

"There is something else you need to know..." Her devil eyes glared into his demon-colored ones, unafraid. "Dominic's like you. He just hasn't shown you yet. He won't go down as easily as Lucifer did. I can promise you that."

Lucca leaned forward, blowing the smoke he had inhaled to float against her soft skin. "Why did you really come here, Katarina?"

"I know your little secret...," she told him, holding it in for just a second longer. "I know you didn't kill *him*."

Amused, he sat back in his chair. "What makes you think that?"

"There's no way you let him die, not after what he did to *her*."

A spark flashed in his eyes for a split second, letting her know she was exactly right. She had seen the way he looked at Chloe, and in a single look she could tell he had fallen for the broken girl at first sight. It was what some would consider true love.

True love shouldn't have existed for them, as it didn't exist for the unlucky ones, but Lucca and Chloe defied the odds, making what they had more than just true love. They could die a thousand deaths only to be reborn to find the other again. Whatever that love was didn't have a name, as it was too powerful to give it one.

He stood and went to the other side of the desk to sit on the edge. "Katarina..."

An image popped into her head. He could so easily lean forward and take her throat in his hands for knowing his secret.

"Would you like to see what is left of him?"

DO YOU BELIEVE IN HEAVEN AND HELL, LUCCA?

The sound of that cold metal door sliding open would haunt her nightmares, and when the light trickled into that dirty dungeon of a room, she could see the body that sat halfway in the shadows.

It was an almost lifeless, mutated, scrawny body that only lived because his captor willed it so, keeping him on the edge of death that was halfway on this living plane and the other in Hell itself.

The image before her would haunt her till the day she died as what she saw shouldn't even exist in fucking nightmares.

"Has Angel seen him yet?" she asked, not crossing the threshold.

"Yes." He confirmed what she thought. "He asked me to keep him alive till his brothers could see him."

She took her eyes off the body to look at him. "You may think you deserve to get to be the one to kill him, but you don't."

"And who do you think does?"

Her eyes went back to the body. "That's for Matthias and Dominic to decide."

Lucca wouldn't ever give her a promise such as that, but at least he heard it.

"Cassius though... you can't let Cassius know he's here...." They all might have devil blood in their veins, but Cassius was the true spawn of the devil. "Because I don't know what he would do if he saw *him* like *this*."

He nodded his head this time, seeming to give her at least that promise.

You could hear the shackles that bound him to the room stir as he started to wake.

"Do you believe in Heaven and Hell, Lucca?"

He thought a moment before he answered her honestly, "I'm not sure anymore."

"It exists." She watched the poor soul scoot deep into the shadows till the only thing you could hear was the rattling of the chains from his fear. "Hell existed in the house I grew up in, but now, you made it exist here."

Lucca smiled. "And Heaven?"

"Heaven exists." Taking one last look, she put her hand on the cold door as she began to slide it closed. "But people like us will never get to see it."

"You didn't want to go closer, so he could see you and you could talk to him?"…

…Kat was in her bedroom in the basement when she heard the door open and feet coming down the steps. She got up from her bed instantly after seeing her brother's face. In her heart she knew something was very wrong.

Dominic wrapped his arms around her, pulling her to him in a huge hug. It was the first time she'd seen him cry as he spoke the words she would never forget. "He's dead. He's finally dead."

Her arms wrapped around him now, gripping him with force as her own tears began to fall. The two stood there together crying for what seemed like an eternity that paled in comparison to the eternity they'd had to spend with their father.

The tears the brother and sister shared weren't for their loss; they were… for their freedom….

…Kat walked away from that door and would never look back. "I wouldn't give him the fucking pleasure."…

…Dominic took her hand and led her up the steps that she would never have to go back down ever again. The weight of their father leaving them the second she closed that basement door.

Taking her down the hall, he opened his bedroom door, and both of them sat down on his bed for the first time.

"You can have my room now. If there's anything you want from yours, we can bring it up her—"

"No," she stopped him harshly before she softened her voice and wiped some more

tears away. "I don't want anything from down there up here."

Understanding, Dominic nodded.

The two sat there in the quiet for a long time seeming to be still numb from the news.

"What do I do now?" she asked, not knowing how to proceed with her own life. It was something she never got to have before. "I don't even know who I am."

His hazel eyes looked into hers, wanting her to grasp something. "You get to be and do whatever you want, Katarina."

Kat looked down at herself, her finger picking up a piece of her pale blond hair. "Can I dye my hair?"

Her brother laughed, putting his arm over her shoulder to pull her close to him. "Yes, if you want."

"What color do you think I should dye it?" she asked, smiling for the first time in what seemed like forever.

"Hmm." Dominic thought for a moment as he stared down at her. "I've always liked you in pink."

WHY CAN'T YOU JUST FUCK M–?

K*atarina came down the steps* with her hair still damp from the shower she'd had to take the second she got home. When she came back, Drago had given her space, somehow instinctively knowing she needed it, but seeing him in the kitchen finishing up his protein shake, she found herself heading toward him.

There was something about the way he was standing there alone that brought an ache to her chest. Walking up behind him, she hesitated before she broke the air of isolation that was so much a part of him. That he hadn't turned around at her approach showed that he was beginning to trust to her. Drago didn't let anyone come up behind his back; he always seemed to be prepared for someone to pull a gun on him.

Sliding her arms around his waist, she didn't feel an ounce of fat underneath the expensive material of his shirt as she laid her cheek on the back of his suit jacket. She expected him to jerk away from her touch, but he didn't.

Drago clamped a hand down on her wrist, pulling her around to face him. The flames in his eyes highlighted the hint of red slumbering in their depths "You okay, Kitty Kat?"

"Yes." She just needed to feel something good.

"What happened to the pink?" he asked, picking up a thick strand of hair that was no longer the pale shade of pink he had always seen but now a pale shade of blond.

Lately, she hadn't been using the pink conditioner in the shower that helped keep it that color. Not seeing one Caruso girl who looked and dressed like her, she'd started to feel more self-conscious of her look. "I thought you might like it better this way."

"I like the blond." He dropped the strand of hair, then leaned down close to her lips. "But I really liked the pink."

Kat smiled as excitement coursed through her veins at being so close to him. She reached up. It was the first time she sought his lips with hers.

He let their kiss only last for a few seconds before his mouth had other plans, going to the base of her throat. His tongue twirled at the pulse that skipped a beat at how good it felt.

Quickly, she realized Drago didn't have to use a gun against his enemies; his tongue was his real weapon. She felt his hands slide down to right below her ass, and found herself wrapping her legs around him as she was abruptly picked up high in the air and taken to the couch, then carefully placed down.

Kat didn't care what he wanted to do to her next, only that he would do something to release the burn that was beginning to hurt between her legs. With her devil eyes staring into his, it was the most erotic thing she had ever experienced as he dragged her shorts and panties down.

Biting down on her bottom lip, she only closed her eyes for a second when the air left her lungs at the suddenness of warm heat latching on to her clit. Startled, she stared down to see Drago's eyes watching her expression as he continued sucking. She felt like maybe she should feel slightly embarrassed to have a man between her legs for the first time, but she wasn't. Instead, what she was letting Drago do only filled her with more pleasure, one she felt she could not escape while her body begged for more.

The red tint on his cheekbones showed that she wasn't the only one affected. Drago might be older and more experienced than her, but that wasn't boredom she saw in his eyes. He watched every movement she made as he dipped his tongue inside of her. Closing her eyes, she wasn't able to watch him as he thrust his tongue inside before pulling it out, then thrusting it inside her again. Fucking her with his tongue, Katarina couldn't prevent the whimpers that left her mouth.

Her body felt boneless, his mouth the only thing keeping her pinned to earth. Each bite, lick, and rub of his tongue made it irresistible to stay right where she was. If she stayed in the same place for the rest of her life, she wanted to stay right there with Drago.

A fissure of desire lanced through her when he inserted a finger inside of her, her thighs splaying wider voluntarily, giving Drago anything he wanted. His mouth lingered over her clit as his finger drove deeper inside of her.

She shuddered when he began moving it inside in a motion that had her biting down on her bottom lip to keep from screaming out loud.

The glide of his finger had her hips rising, yet again wanting more than he was giving her. The tingling ache was getting stronger and fiercer, building to a point she wasn't sure she could withstand.

"Drago!" Moaning, she twisted and turned as her nails tore at his hair. She didn't want him to stop. What she did want was more, and Drago wasn't giving it to her.

A swipe of his tongue on her clit had her shouting at him, "Please. . . ."

His eyes flashed back to hers as his tongue swiped over her clit again, this time much slower.

That swipe had her bunching his hair in her hands.

Easing his fingers out of her, then pushing them inside again as he played with her clit was more than she could take. Strong pulses rippled through her channel as her muscles clamped down on his fingers as her climax consumed what was left of her thoughts, whirling her in a dance of desire that Drago expertly guided her through step-by-step.

It was only when he removed his fingers and mouth from her body that she realized it was over. Blinking at him dazedly, she watched as he stood up.

He's not going to do this to me again, is he?!

She was still blinking at him soundlessly as he went to the kitchen sink to wash his hands.

Why can't you just fuck m—?

BACK OUT THE RABBIT HOLE

L*ying in bed next to* him, she felt an ache in her heart at seeing the small space between them. It was only a couple of inches that separated them, but it felt like a mile.

He had told her it was late and that they needed to get some rest, but she couldn't help but feel there was a reason why he abruptly stopped himself from touching her—again.

Katarina had been willing to give herself to him, but he didn't want to take it.

She wondered if she needed to help him take it. She had just been lying there, after all, while he was the one who gifted out the pleasure. That was probably what bugged her about it the most. She wanted him to *feel* what she *felt,* and he wasn't even giving it a chance.

She scooted over closer to him. She was inexperienced, sure, but she didn't think it should be that hard to push him over the edge. He'd already almost been there twice, only seeming to stop himself the second before it was too late.

Drago was still awake, reaching out to wrap an arm around her waist when he felt her body come up next to his.

Her hand went to his solid chest feeling the strong muscles underneath, causing her desire that she'd felt for him earlier to come back full force. She placed her lips on his neck, finding the warm skin in the dark of the night, giving just a sweet kiss at first, before the wetness of her tongue replaced that innocent one.

Those muscles under her hand instantly tensed. Taking it as a sign she was doing something right, she tried to go lower but was stopped by the strong arm holding her tightly in place.

His voice came out more as a growl. "What are you doing, Katarina?"

"I just wanted to return the favor," she told him, placing another kiss on his neck.

Drago moved out from being slightly underneath her, sitting up on the edge of the bed to rub his hands in his hair.

She couldn't help but feel like she'd done something wrong, and she didn't like that feeling. Unable to take being dissed any longer, she sat up as well, only coming to two conclusions as to why he was doing this. "Is it because I'm a Luciano or because you don't like the way I look?"

He shook his head. "It's neither of those."

"Oh." She took a breath, somewhat relieved. She had prepared herself for one of those two options which seemed like they would hurt the most. Licking her dry lips, she almost didn't want to ask.... "Then what is it?"

He took a long, deep breath, finally coming out with it. "You're too young—"

"I see." She stopped him and got out of the bed, unable to be around him a second longer. "Too young to fuck, but not too young to marry."

"Wha—" Drago quickly stood when he saw her get to the top of the steps. "Where the hell are you going?"

Flying down the steps, she yelled at him without turning back, "Home. I need to see my brothers."

"It's the middle of the fucking night! How are you supposed to get there?"

"Angel will take me," she barked back, almost making it to the door. She would borrow some of Adalyn's shoes.

"Kat!" He ran after her, but she was too quick. As he watched her hand reach for the door, his voice seemed to change. "Please!"

She opened the door. She should have known that they would go back to being at each other's throats—it was too easy to go back out the rabbit hole eventually.

"Don't do this, please."

She stopped in her tracks, hearing the change in his voice now.

"I promise you, I will take you to see your brothers tomorrow, and if you want to stay there, you can. I won't make you come back with me," he promised her wholeheartedly. Drago held out his hand, not taking another step toward her, letting it be her decision to make. "Come back."

Kat thought for a moment, not knowing what to do.

His voice was heavy. "Just let me hold you for one night."

She squeezed her eyes shut holding her breath till she released it slowly, closing the door as she stood on the same side as her husband.

Drago's breath released as well while she walked toward him. Reaching out, he scooped her up like he had earlier, letting her legs wrap around him.

Holding him tightly, she didn't let herself cry as he carried her all the way up the steps and placed her back onto the bed.

He set her right on the edge, leaning down in front of her, going to his knees, so he could look her right in the eyes. "I need you to listen to me, Katarina."

Nodding her head, she could see the pure need in the red ring in his eyes.

"You're too young. So young I shouldn't have picked you," he told her, then tried again. "I took you away before you even had a chance to decide what you wanted to do for the rest of your life, and I feel so fucking guilty for that."

Kat continued to listen, hearing the pain in his voice.

"I already feel so fucking guilty for marrying you. How am I supposed to look at myself when I finally let myself have you? When I only picked you out of revenge."

Reaching a hand out, she cupped his tanned face, letting her thumb rub over the shadows under his eyes. "I know why you picked me," she told him, letting him know it was no secret. "But we both did what we had to do for *our* families." They got to be the ones to bring peace between them, *and there is no greater job than that.*

"It doesn't change how old you are, Katarina." He pushed his head deeper into her hand.

Kat didn't like that the age thing bothered him when that wasn't even a thought in her mind. "No, but the things I've been through, the things I've seen make me much older than what I am on the outside."

The shadows in his face grew deeper. "That's another reason why I hate myself. I took you, and I don't even know what you've been through."

Dropping her hand from his face, she took a deep breath to tell him what only a few souls on this earth knew. "My father didn't want me based on one reason alone: I was born a girl. I'm here only because Dominic somehow managed to get him to keep me, but it was my older brothers who raised me. I was kept out of sight in the basement, only coming out for school or if he needed me to do his books or count money."

It must have been hard for Drago to hear, but he stayed right there wanting to listen to every word with the fire in his eyes raging brighter.

"It was actually safer to be in the basement, and I had it much easier than my brothers did living up there with him. Dominic made it *almost* impossible for him to get to me early on, but then, when he found out I had a gift, Lucifer didn't hit me anymore. He was too afraid that I could hurt my head, and his calculator would be gone. So, then I was just forced to watch him hit my brothers... again... and again... and again."

That turned out to be much harder than taking any hit her father had to give.

"That's enough for tonight." He stopped her when he saw the first tear fall. Drago picked her up, taking them to the bed, so he could wrap his arms around her and hold her. "You have the remainder of our lives to tell me the rest—if you stay with me."

Trying to stop her tears, she pressed her body deeper into his, feeling the cold metal of his ring that touched her skin. For the first time, she finally noticed the weight of her own that sat snuggly around her finger…

To have and to hold, from this day forward, for better, for worse, for richer, for poorer, in sickness and in health, until death do us part.

She had no intentions of dying or taking it off anytime soon. *Not ever.*

THE SINS OF MY FATHER

S*he was glad Drago was* with her because she thought walking up to that house would have made her happy, but it didn't. She was happy to get to see her brothers, but she wasn't happy to be home. Coming back, she could see it for what it was: a house of horrors.

The devil might not live in it anymore, but you couldn't take back what happened in that house.

Dominic opened the door as soon as their feet touched the porch, the sight of him causing Kat to jump up into his arms to give him a hug. It was the longest time they had spent away from each other; she was so glad to see him again. "I missed you so much."

"I missed you too." He hugged her for a bit before he placed her back down on the floor.

It didn't take her long to figure out that something seemed off about her brother. She knew he was just as glad to see her, but she could see the silent rage he carried behind his hazel eyes.

"Kat, why don't you go see Matthias. I want to talk to Drago."

Swallowing hard, she looked at Drago, not wanting to leave, but he gave her nod telling her it was okay. So, she did, knowing that Drago was perfectly capable of taking care of himself.

As she walked down the hall, it was hard for her to pass the basement door, unable to even look at it as she continued to Matthias's room. She knocked on the door first, but when she got no response, she cracked it open to find Matthias on the bed just lying there silently, staring at the wall.

Kat went in doing what she usually did when she saw him like this. Slowly, she lay down beside him, placing her hands under her face to where he could no longer see that wall and was forced to stare only at her.

His haunted eyes seemed to finally see her as he slowly came back from the darkness. Whispering, his voice sounded just as haunted. "Hi, Kat."

"Hi." She smiled at him knowing he always liked it when she smiled.

"What are you doing here?"

"I wanted to see you." She reached out to feel his face. "You didn't think I forgot about you, did you?"

The way he looked at her fucking killed her. It was almost like he wasn't even there, slowly becoming a shell of a man who had been hurt too many times.

She tried her best to keep her happy face. "You know, Angel lives just a few doors down from me. You can come over to visit anytime you want now."

He only nodded.

Kat could no longer hold her smile. It hurt too much to see him this far gone. "I love you, Matthias."

"I love you too," he whispered more clearly, his eyes less glazed as they watched the tear fall from the corner of her eye and down to her hand under her head. "Don't cry, Kat."

What she had said seemed to work to get him out of that dark place for now, *but what about next time?*

"I'll be okay," he tried to promise her. "Why don't you go find Cassius. I think something has been bothering him, but he won't tell me what it is."

Kat stared at him for a moment longer, not wanting to leave him but also knowing she would never be the one to save him. Placing a kiss on his forehead, she regretfully left him to find Cassius.

Going up the creaky old stairs at the back of the house, she knew exactly where he'd be. The upstairs consisted of Lucifer's old room, but Dominic used it now after he had given her his old room. She opened the big window, letting the cold air hit her face.

"You know I don't like it when you come out here," Kat grumbled, squeezing out the window to sit on the roof next to her youngest brother.

Cassius kept quietly staring out at the rough exterior of the rundown neighborhood they lived in.

"What's wrong?" she asked worriedly. She'd never really seen him this way before. She had only ever seen him upset once, and that was when Drago had chosen her.

The young boy flexed his jaw tightly. "Dom's been pissed since you left. He's acting like he's going to fuckin' kill somebody."

Her mouth going dry wasn't from the cold wind. A shiver shook her whole core, unsure if she wanted to know, but she didn't have a choice but to ask... "Who?"

Drago watched Katarina walk away until she disappeared. Once she did, Dominic wasted no time speaking his mind.

"I was so fucking careful," the Luciano boss's voice cut like a knife into the dead air. "So fucking careful to not let you Carusos know we had a sister, and somehow *he* found out."

A part of him felt bad for Katarina's brother. It was obvious he felt as if he had failed his sister. He just didn't quite get the scope of whom exactly he was up against. "You'll come to find out Lucca always knows everything."

But then again, he assumed Dominic now did.

"It's quite annoying, really," Drago continued, finally glad to face his guilt head on. "But it's not him you should be mad at. I'm the one who chose her, and for that... I'm sorry."

Dominic looked at him with a flex in his jaw.

"I want you to know, choosing Katarina had nothing to do with *her* and everything to do with *you*. I wanted you to hurt for what your father did to me. She just happened to be in the way."

That flex in his jaw seemed to relax slightly.

He began to show Dominic that any hatred he had toward him, didn't compare to the hatred Drago had towards himself. "Sometimes it's hard for me to look at her, to know that I used her."

"Good." Dominic's fierce hazel eyes pierced his soul. "I've had to wake up every fucking day for the last seventeen years paying for the sins of my father, and I'm glad to know I won't be the only one anymore."

"No, you won't," he agreed.

Feeling the release of some of his guilt, he had wanted to talk to Dominic ever since his feelings for Kat consumed him. Both of them coming to a silent agreement helped, but there was one last thing he needed to do. "Can you show me the basement?"

Nodding, Dominic didn't even have to ask why he needed to see it as he led him down a hall, taking him to the door that opened to the descending staircase.

Drago walked down it, not knowing till he finally saw it that what he would see would be something he would never forget. It was a cold concrete room that sat under the house, used to hold old things, but up against the wall in the middle of it sat a cozy pink rug. There was a single bed by a heater, a little nightstand with a lamp on top. Even a poster of flowers hung above, creating a little room that wouldn't look so bad if it weren't surrounded by the cold concrete.

It was what it was, a basement that was forced to hold a room for a little girl.

"It won't get any easier…." Dominic's grave voice echoed

through the space.

Looking back at him, Drago saw only the man who'd raised Katarina. "What won't?"

"Looking at her."

Drago's eyes went back to the makeshift room, seeing what he had missed the first time... It had been made with love.

"Anybody," Cassius told her. "He thinks Lucca knew about you before they came in, and he doesn't understand how he found out."

"Oh." She scooted closer to her brother, so she could put her arm around his shoulder. "He's just upset, Cass. I'll talk to him and tell him to take it easy."

Cassius continued to stare out at the trash-filled land.

It was never like talking to a young teenager when she talked to her youngest brother, with their talks consisting of mature material most of the time. She had always tried to keep him on the side with her and her older brothers, *the good side,* and away from their father's, *the bad side.* But... he was so much like Lucifer.

She could always see the battle of good and evil in his head, the devilish boy being talked back off that line before he crossed it, and it couldn't be undone. Except this time. Something was different.

"What happened?" she asked, terrified, afraid that she was too late. The crime looked like it had already been committed.

Cassius finally looked at her with his malevolent eyes. "I did something, Kat, and I don't think you'll never forgive me."...

...At a very young age, Cassius wandered out the house when no one was looking, which happened too often because of all the fighting.

The sky was dark, but that didn't stop him. His little legs always walked in the same direction, going to the dirty park that hardly any kids played at anymore.

This time, no kids were there when he arrived, too late at night, only some sketchy people who were huddled under blankets by some torn-down fencing.

Little Cassius took a seat on the swing, always wishing someone would push him to help get him started. Instead, he always ended just sitting there, not using the swing for its purpose.

The stars and the moon were the only light he had, but he could see the eight-legged creature running on the ground underneath him.

Without even thinking, his little shoe came down carefully, smashing only half of the spider.

Cassius stared down at it, watching four of its legs continue to move for several minutes... enjoying it. He turned only when the jingle of the swing beside him could be heard.

He thought it might've been Dominic at first, but quickly he learned it wasn't.

The stranger took a seat beside him. "Hello."

Cassius stared at the guy, unafraid. He wasn't scared of anything, really, not even strangers. "Hi."

"What's your name?"

Everyone always seemed to know who he was in the neighborhood, but he had never seen this man before, and he felt like he would have remembered him, since he didn't look like anyone around here. "Cassius."

Swinging slightly, he smiled at the boy. "It's nice to meet you, Cassius."

Little Cassius went back to looking at the spider that was still trying to move.

"What are you doing out here so late?"

He told the stranger why he always came out here all alone. "My father is trying hurt Kat again."

"Who's Kat?" he asked, looking down to see what the boy was staring at.

"My sister."

"Oh." The stranger stood then, going in front of the little boy before he crouched down, so Cassius would look at him. "I like to hurt things too."

"You do?" Cassius moved his eyes away from the tortured spider to look at the stranger who seemed to be somewhere around his brother Dominic's age. He was either not yet an adult or barely one at all.

"Yes." His intense blue-green eyes shifted between the two colors in the moonlight. "But..." The young stranger stood up, squashing the spider, so it could meet his death. "...they must deserve it."

"Why?" Cassius asked, unable to look away from him anymore.

"Because if we're not careful, we will end up hurting people like your sister."

The little boy shook his head, becoming worried. "I don't want to hurt Kat."

"I won't let you," the stranger assured him. "I can help you."

"Okay." Cassius smiled up at his new friend. "What's your name?"

Going behind the swing, he started pushing the little boy. "You can call me... Luke."...

..."I didn't know it was him, Kat." Cassius shook his head angrily. "I didn't know my friend was fuckin Lucca the whole time...."

Katarina's body and mind were numb, still in shock over what her brother had told her.

"...Not till he walked in our front door that day."

THE DAY KATARINA WAS CHOSEN

*"You promised me!" **Katarina screamed** at her brother, uncaring of the many women who stood in their living room. "You promised me I wouldn't have to go back down there ever again!"*

"I know," Dominic told her painfully and regretfully. "But, please, it's only for a little bit."

Kat shook her head strongly, trying not to cry. "No."

"They're here," Matthais yelled from the window, seeing the black Cadillacs pull up.

"He will choose you if he sees you, I know it." Dominic's voice started to break. "There will be nothing I can do. They'll kill Angel if I don't let them have you."

Tears started to fall down her cheeks one after the other.

"Please, Kat, I can't lose you." He cried, taking her into his arms.

Taking a breath, she nodded into his chest.

"Hurry," Dominic told her, opening the door. "Keep all the lights off, and as soon as they leave, I'll come down to get you."

With each step down those godforsaken steps, she cried more and more. It took her back to a time and place she'd felt weak. Like she was still living under Lucifer's roof, still under his control. It was like the months since his death of becoming the strong and smart woman she was meant to be hadn't even happened.

Kat ran to the only part of the basement that felt safe, sitting down on the pink fuzzy carpet Dominic had brought home to her when she was young. She placed her back on her old bed as she held her knees to her chest, silently waiting for her brother to come down here and free her once again.

"Meow." Shadow rubbed his black fur against her, making loud purring sounds to get her to pet him. "Meow."

She ran a hand along his back, distracting herself from the dark basement the more she petted him. She didn't know how long she had been down there when the door at the top of the steps opened, bringing light into the basement.

Kat had heard her brother come down those steps many times over the last seventeen years, but the feet that came down them now weren't Dominic's. Her breath caught in her throat as her heart started to pound out of her chest, unable to find the strength in herself to hide under her bed.

When she saw the shadowy figure reach the bottom of the steps, all she could look at were those blue-green glowing orbs that somehow seemed to have their own light source behind them.

The figure stepped closer, giving her a better look.

Katarina hadn't been in Lucifer's presence for months, but the way she felt looking at him was no different than how she'd felt when she used to look at her father. The devil might've been dead, but a demon still walked this city, and even if she had hidden like she should've, she knew there was no hiding from whoever the hell he was.

She watched him stretch out a cold hand, knowing it was cold from the callous tone in his voice that turned her warm-bloodied veins into ice.

"Come with me, darlin'."...

...Going back to the day Katarina was chosen, she realized now Lucca had known about everything. Before he had ever come down those steps.

This whole time...

She knew that Cassius had more than likely confided in him about what went on in their house.

"I'm so sorry, Kat," Cassius told her again, still angrily shaking his head at himself.

She squeezed her brother as hard as she could in a hug, doing it even though she knew Cassius hated it. "There's nothing to be sorry about." Kat squeezed him even harder, smiling at the thought that Lucca had been doing what she had been trying to do with her brother over the years. "I'm actually grateful."

And she truly fucking was.

They spent the whole day with her brothers, Drago only getting up to leave when it was well past the sun going down.

Putting on his coat, he looked at her and held out his hand for her to take. "You coming, Kat?"

She knew what those words meant; he had kept his promise. He had taken her back home, and if she wanted to stay, then he'd let her. It was her decision to make.

Kat looked at Dominic first. He gave her a nod that reminded her of what he had told her.

You get to be and do whatever you want, Katarina.

Her eyes then went around the house. The wicked memories she had in the home charred the walls from the hell it once was. The devil was gone, but the burnt walls remained.

It took Kat leaving this house to realize she would never become the woman she was supposed to be if she stayed in these two thousand five hundred and fifty-six square feet.

I have a fucking family to save.

Getting up, she took Drago's warm hand, thanking God for the cold one that had shown her what she should be.

Falling in love was a scary thing that he had hoped he would never experience after watching Lucca fall for Chloe.

It seemed more painful to love someone so much than it looked pleasurable. Seeming to only lead to heartbreak.

It all didn't make sense till her hand touched his. The only way to understand falling in love was when you had already fallen, and it was too late to ever get back up.

That dark black hole you thought was bleak looking in was

actually a wonderland once you hit the bottom.

The hole he had fallen in was extra special, because Katarina was so special.

He had thought there were no such things as true heroes. His world of crime had kept him from thinking so, the only heroes were the anti-heroes who balanced out all the noble things with sins.

For the first time, it wasn't the girl who *needed* saving; it was the girl who *did* the saving. This story had only one hero… and it wasn't the name on this book.

THE TRUTH SHALL ALWAYS SET YOU FREE

W*alking through the casino, she* walked hand in hand with Drago, feeling lighter and lighter the closer she got to their apartment door.

There was only one scar left that hadn't started to heal, only one stone left unturned, and she only hoped that one day very soon he would be ready to see her.

Seconds away from getting onto the closing elevator that was full of people, Kat's shoulder was hit by another who bumped into her so hard it caused her hand to fall out of Drago's.

"Excuse you." She snapped over her shoulder trying to get a look at the person she hadn't paid attention to as he passed, but there were so many people it was impossible to tell who it had been.

Her head turning back to the front, she saw Drago's back entering the elevator as it quickly slid to a close. It wasn't until the door closed that fear kick in.

"What did you say?" Drago asked turning to see what she had said, but when he turned there was no Kat. With only an inch of space left for the elevator doors to close, he could see her black eye just on the other side before that inch of space disappeared.

"Kat!" Quickly, Drago went for the elevator buttons before it could go up, but it was so full he had to practically shove a person to the ground to get to it fast enough.

Pressing the button for the door to open again, it was too late as it began its journey up.

"KAT!"

Fear setting into his bones, he pressed the next floor button, so he could get off and take the stairs back down, but what had seemed to go so fast now seemed to go so slow…

Slowly Kat's feet stepped back, something wasn't right and she felt like she was right where the killer wanted her to be.

What the—!

Her body was snatched back as she was pulled into a stairwell.

It wasn't till she was pushed against the wall did she finally face who Lucca had called One-Shot.

No, please, not you....

The shock had kept her from screaming at first but the hand that covered her mouth roughly was now keeping it that way.

Don't do this... she pleaded with her eyes, looking into the blueish-black depths... *Please Sal.*

Kat tried to fight harder to get free but he had her pinned so perfectly that she could barely budge. Hearing the feet running down the steps, she thought she had been saved when Drago came into view. *Oh thank Go—*

"Black hoodie and sunglasses at three o'clock." Sal quickly told him over his shoulder.

Drago had only caught her eyes for a second before he walked right out leaving her to die.

NO! He's right here!!!! It's Sal!!!!! She had wanted to scream at him but the hand kept her from doing so. *Come back!!*

Once that stairwell door was closed, Kat knew for sure this time was it. Always secretly knowing it would be her own flesh and blood that was going to be the death of her... she just didn't think it would be at the hand of a brother, but she should have realized that he might not have considered her a sister when he had yet to even try to see her.

His hand finally peeling off her face, she prepared herself to scream....

"I'm sorry...," Sal told her.

AH!-Huh? That scream didn't come out as she felt his arms wrap around her and she was being hugged to him.

"I didn't mean to scare you," he continued hugging her. "But I couldn't risk him hearing us in here."

She stood their rigidly in his arms. "So… you're not trying to kill me?"

"No." He laughed.

"Thank God." Instantly all the tension left her body as she lifted her arms up to wrap them around him. It was an indescribable feeling she got being finally able to meet the brother she had been robbed of. The brother she felt like she would have been most similar to.

"Kat, I want you to know that even though I haven't let you see me yet, I promise you, I've been there."

"You have?" she asked, holding him tighter and becoming teary eyed.

"I have," her brother assured her. "I was just afraid of not only letting you know, but One-Shot."

"It's okay." Kat was the one to have to assure him now letting him know she not only understood his reasoning for ignoring her but that it simply didn't matter. They were finally together and that was all she could ask for.

The door flying open had them turning to see a furious Drago coming in; not saying a word, he pulled Kat into his arms.

The kisses he was showering her with, she didn't feel the need to tell him that she thought his ass had left her to die.

"Well?" Sal asked waiting to hear what had happened.

Drago gave her one last kiss, before he regretfully shook his head…. "He's gone."

Lucca practically kicked open the door, not understanding how One-Shot kept besting him. He knew everyone and everything all except for something as important as the man that he felt was trying to take him down. That was what led him here; there was only one man that stood between him and this city becoming his, and right now he was staring at him.

"Oh good." Dante didn't even jump at his forced entrance into his office. "You were just who I wanted to talk to."

Staring down his father, that he had pictured killing a million times, it was everything he could do to get him to keep from doing it. "Is that so?"

His ice-blue eyes stared back at him, knowing exactly what his son was doing to him in his head. "What makes you think you can hire Katarina without my permission? She's not only a Luciano, but she's not even a soldier for Christ's sake."

Lucca knew what he meant by soldier, it was his way of fucking saying she wasn't a man. "You've seem to forgotten that she's married now, making Katarina a Caruso."

Dante swung back the last bit of his whiskey before he slammed down the glass causing it to break. "I don't give a fuck if the girl is fucking Drago. She's still the daughter of Lucifer, and that job belongs to one of my *men* if you can't handle it any longer!"

There it is. The truth shall always set you free.

"That job belongs to Katarina and her alone." His tone might have not have matched his father's but his intense blue-green eyes did. "And if you continue speaking that way about the wife of one of our most loyal De Santis men, I will have no choice but to let our men think you're One-Shot."

Dante rose to his feet. "That's why you're here isn't it? You've come to see if he's me."

Silence from his firstborn gave him his answer.

"Just because you want it to be me, doesn't make him me, my son."

"No," Lucca agreed with an almost sigh. "But I could always hope."

"I should fucking kill you." Dante spat sitting back down in his chair, the monster he had made becoming more evident with every passing day.

"Be careful, Father, I can always make *my* men believe One-Shot is you." Leaving, Lucca could never resist parting without a promise. "Your times almost up, old man."

As he closed the door, his father's voice could still be heard on the other side.

"God help us all."

"Lake's been watching this show a lot lately, and it's starting to scare me," Vincent told them with a bit of worry in his voice.

"Is it *Deadly Women*? Because Elle's been watching that too," Nero agreed, looking a bit frightful his sweet girlfriend would watch that.

Lucca looked at him, usually not involving himself with them in talking about Chloe, but it seemed like a lightbulb had gone off when he heard the name. "Chloe has too."

"It's creepy as hell." Vincent shook a little. "When did they start watching that?"

"I don't know…," Nero admitted.

Drago and Angel looked at each other, both of them knowing the source.

Vincent looked at Angel. "Is Adalyn watching it?"

"No, I don't think so."

Drago rolled his eyes at the horrible lie.

"How about Katarina?" Lucca asked with a smile, seeming to now know why his scarred beauty had become interested in a show like that.

Deciding not to answer, Drago looked down at the men. "You pussies aren't scared your girls are going to kill you in your sleep, are you?"

"Hell yes, I am," Vincent answered, like he had asked a dumbass question. "And the way your wife took a fucking bat to your house, you should too!"

"I'm not scared." Drago sat back in his chair. "I got rid of the bat and hid my gun from her."

"Smart man." The pretty boy nodded his head. "Kat's hot as hell, but her ass is fucking crazier than Lake's."

Angel reached out and punched him in the arm.

"What the fuck!" Vincent growled. "You're dating my sister,

dumbass. You can't hit me when you think the same thing!"

"No." Drago hit his other arm harder than the tatted one had. "But I can."

The pretty boy growled even louder, standing up from his chair. "What the fuck!"

"Sit your ass back down," Lucca demanded. "You're not going to fight Drago."

"You're right." Vincent sat back down knowing what he said was true. "I wouldn't want to hurt my face now that I'm the good-looking one again."

Maria, who had been trying to ignore them, practically choked. "Hah! Yeah, right."

"It's true. Kat said I was pretty, and I haven't seen her swooning over Lucca like the rest of the girls have."

The only thing that stopped Drago from wringing his neck was his underboss's hand on his chest.

Lucca's eyes glowered at the soldier he hated most. "You don't get to kill him. I've already called him."

"Why do you keep forgetting that she also called you a dumbass?" Maria taunted the pretty boy, wanting Lucca to do it already.

"She did call you a dumbass," Amo agreed, finally speaking.

"All I heard was pretty," Vincent corrected them before he glowered his own eyes at the tall blonde. "Why are you in here anyway—"

"She has more fucking right to be in here than you," Lucca's voice cut him off. It appeared like he was about to kill him when the door finally opened, saving the pretty boy's life just in time.

"Sorry I'm late," Sal came in. "Me and Kat were having a debate about the Pythagorean theorem."

"Nerds." Vincent practically gagged the word up before a huge slap hit the back of his head. Turning to see it was Sal who hit him, his pretty mouth snapped shut.

It took everything Drago had not to laugh, it was obvious Vincent feared Sal the most, having good reason to do so. There was nothing like having the control of being able to hack into any phone or computer to find out everything about a person and their deepest darkest secrets to keep a man, even as annoying as Vincent, afraid. Making him one hell of a powerful man just by sitting behind a keyboard. That was fucking true power.

"Now that were all here,"—Lucca flipped his lighter open to take a much-needed hit off a cigarette—"look around to the people in this room."

Eyeing around the room, he saw everyone's face turned serious, the boardroom they were in quickly turning into a war room with just a few words.

"These are the only faces you can trust," their underboss continued commanding each and every one. "Anyone outside, we cannot trust isn't One-Shot. *No matter who it is.*"

Solemnly, every soldier nodded their head, fully understanding that he was suspecting a Caruso to be behind the curtain.

"One-Shot might be gone for now but he will return… and when he does, the only one who will deal with him—" Looking at each and every one of them, Lucca staked his claim. "—is me."

THIS TUB IS BIG ENOUGH FOR TWO

It had been one whole month since she had married Drago, and it really had been wedded bliss… *besides the whole killer thing that is.* If and when One-Shot returned they would deal with it together, because being together came easy for them. You wouldn't have even known it was an arranged marriage, both Katarina and Drago easily forgetting.

She was happier than she had ever been, getting to see her brothers whenever she wanted, having a group of girlfriends, a husband she enjoyed spending time with, and she also had a job in two families that knew her worth.

"Bye, Amo." She waved at him once she reached her door.

"Later, Kat."

Katarina could smell the food that was cooking on the other

side. When she opened the door, she found Drago cooking what looked like spaghetti. Going over to him, she was thankful the big meatballs he had made were the only protein.

Pulling her to him, he gave her a kiss. "How was work?"

"Good." She smiled, kissing him back.

"I ran you a bath." Drago pushed her pink hair behind her ear. "I'll let you know when the food is done."

"You just gave me another reason for having a husband."

He laughed. "What's the other reason?"

"Having someone to toast my Pop-Tarts for me."

"I don't toast them for you." He seemed confused.

"No." Kat gave him a wink. "But now you know."

Drago's tough face softened. "Yes, I do."

Excited for her bath, she went up the stairs, and when she reached the bathroom, she saw the huge tub was waiting with bubbles floating on top. Throwing her hair up in a bun, she practically ripped off all her clothes before she slowly got in.

Blissfully, she felt the water surround her.

My husband isn't so bad after all.

Katarina rested on the back of the tub, letting the soothing warmth of the water relax her muscles as she closed her eyes. She didn't realize she had dozed off, not hearing him call her name till Drago opened the door to make sure she was all right.

Awake now, she could see that ring of fire beginning to burn brighter in his eyes upon seeing her. He hadn't touched her since that last time, and she didn't force him, wanting him to come to terms with the guilt he carried on his own. Dreamily, she swirled the bubbles to cover the tips of her breast that were poking through the scented water.

Drago stalked closer and closer till he towered over her and the tub.

She looked up at him. He was so handsome that she had to lick her dry lips.

He lowered himself, going down to his knees as he reached out to rub his thumb over her bottom lip she had just licked. "Better be careful, Kitty Kat, before you poke the bear."

"Really?" she asked before she did it again.

Trailing down from her lips to her neck, his finger slid down between her breasts. "Yes."

"You're getting your shirt wet," Kat teased before he got much further.

Disappointed, she saw his hand come out of the water. She expected him to leave and was surprised to see Drago unbuttoning his shirt and slinging it toward the hamper to the side of the tub. His hand dipped back into the water, returning to the spot he had left.

When Drago's hand slid down her belly, warmth flooded inside, becoming warmer than the water surrounding her. The quivering ache came next, making her glad that he couldn't see under the water. Her hands went to the sides of the bathtub to hold herself upright, afraid that she would drown if she didn't.

Her hands gripped the tub tighter the lower he got as he ran his fingertips along the inner length of her thigh. She forgot about swirling the bubbles, letting the sensations that Drago was arousing within her envelope her into its steamy mist. She inhaled the fragrant bath oil that Drago must have put in the water. Her elbows sloshed water over the side when his fingers came close to her essence before teasingly gliding away. Back and forth his hand wandered over her skin. Each time he touched her sex, his fingers would linger longer before pulling away.

Unable to take it anymore when a knuckle pushed down on her clit, she grabbed his wrist to hold it in place.

Drago twisted his hand free, sliding his fingers through her cleft to her opening, gliding inside so smoothly it didn't even cause a ripple in the water. Her toes clenched when he licked the curve of her shoulder as his finger roved higher. More water sloshed over the side when his movements became faster and harder.

The only part of his body that was touching her was his hand, and it wasn't enough.

"Drago, I need…."

"I know what you need." His low voice sent shivers up her spine. Risking drowning, she released the side of the tub to run her hands over his chest. Curls of hair tickled her palms as she self-indulgently touched Drago. She loved being able to touch him, feeling the pounding of his heart underneath her hand. It was a power trip that had her thighs clenching on the hand that was touching her intimately. That somehow, she was in control of the large dangerous man who everyone feared would take them out. She knew he would stop the second she told him to; the gentleness he was touching her with showed that and more. It was a loving touch that was centered on her pleasure without asking anything for himself.

His skin was damp from the steam of the water, and his harsh face showed the torture he was going through to restrain himself.

Leaning forward, she placed a sweet kiss above his heart, sending more water over the edge as Drago's hand jerked in reaction.

"This tub is big enough for two." She moaned as her hands went to his shoulders, trying to pull him in the water with her forgetting that he still had his pants and shoes on. She just wanted to be able to touch every inch of him, and the tub was providing him a barrier from the needs that were swamping her.

He shook his head, pulling his hand away from her to come up out of the water to hold her chin. "I can't do that."

"Why?" she pleaded with her eyes, afraid he was going to leave her in need again.

"Because I have something I need to ask you."

Kat looked at him confused for a second, but when his dry hand came up from his pocket holding a ring, she stared at the beautiful platinum metal that matched her wedding ring. This ring, however, held a beautiful black diamond.

"Will you marry me?" Drago asked, his voice heavy. "I want to marry you for real this time. Not because someone told us to, but because I love you."

Tears flooded her eyes. She hadn't thought she'd ever be the girl who would be gushy when a man asked her to marry him. It was a moment that she hadn't been given before, and now here Drago was, giving her that moment, making it all the more special as they were already legally wed and wed in God's eyes.

"Of course," she cried, letting Drago take her left hand to slide on the beautiful ring that she couldn't have picked better herself.

She wanted to jump out of the water or pull him in, but her husband made the choice for her as he reached for a large towel and lifted her into the cocooning warmth. Standing her on her feet, he used the towel to dry her, not even missing the sole of her feet, murmuring to her how beautiful his wife was with every spot he dried. Being pampered and spoiled wasn't what she was used to, but it was *soooo* nice she never wanted it to end.

It didn't, as she was picked up and brought to their bed.

Knowing that she was about to get her wish she wanted fulfilled, her heart raced till his lips came down on hers, slowing her pounding heart back down.

That was all she needed to writhe underneath him. She became pliable in his arms, following every direction he wanted. It was evident in both their eyes that this time wasn't going to be slow and sweet, both of them in too much need for that.

"I promise to fuck you slowly next time," he growled, covering her with his huge frame.

Feeling the steady pressure of his dick filling her, she willingly tilted her hips upward at the urging of his hands cupping her bottom. Uncaring of how he fucked her as long as he did.

When Drago moaned out for her to stay still, she froze, experiencing the building pressure within her and ignoring the instincts that told her to thrust back against him. It was a dance in which Drago led her where he wanted her to go. Each stroke and thrust of his body into hers sent spiraling peaks of desire that traveled all the way down to her toes.

She curved her body against his, her knees gripping each side of his hips as they moved slickly together. Drago's rocking motions began to speed up, and Katrina wasn't sure she would be able to keep up. His gentler movements became harder, firmer, the mouth on her breast leaving to catch hers in a kiss that stole what little oxygen she had left.

On a hard thrust, she felt the mysterious climax she had read about in books, making the other ones she'd had pale in comparison to this. It ripped through her in waves of pleasure that she would have never believed if she hadn't experienced it for herself. Drago's loud moan being the only thing that dragged her back to earth, running her hands over his shoulders and down his back as he shook in her arms. If she hadn't watched, she would have missed the expression on his face, and it was one she would always remember.

Reaching up, she cupped his face, her thumb rubbing over the shadows that were almost gone. "I love you too."

SO LONG AS YOU BOTH SHALL LIVE

K*at stood on the beach* holding her husband's hand. He had surprised her by whisking her away for a week, so they could have a honeymoon.

A man with leis around his neck began to speak. "Katarina, do you take Drago to be your wedded husband to live together in marriage? Do you promise to love him, comfort him, honor and keep him for better or worse, for richer or poorer, in sickness and health, and forsaking all others, be faithful only to him so long as you both shall live?"

And to get married, as Drago had called it, *for real this time.*

She also planned to surprise him with a gift of her own later tonight, deciding to finally take the De Santis name. However, Kat wouldn't be leaving her old name behind. It had taken too long to finally be proud to bear the Luciano name and she wasn't giving that up now. Katarina Luciano-De Santis, sounded like a badass name that she deserved.

Smiling up at him, she didn't have to choke the words out this time. "I do."

"And do you, Drago, take Katarina to be your wedded wife, to live together in marriage? Do you promise to love her, comfort her, honor and keep her for better or worse, for richer or poorer, in sickness and health, and forsaking all others, be faithful only to her, for as long as you both shall live?"

Drago's fierce but loving eyes stared back at her, matching the red wedding dress she had wanted to wear just for that reason. "I do."

YOU

There isn't much that could keep me from you,
Not even the hateful words you spew.
Not even the mark on my face
Not even the tears I shed.

There is so much that should keep me from you,
But my mouth stays quiet
My feet stand still
Until I am ready
To part from
You.

Sarah Brianne

Please, if you or someone you know ever needs help, follow this link to get more information and help.

YOU ARE NOT ALONE.

www.victimsofcrime.org/help-for-crime-victims
/national-hotlines-and-helpful-links

Printed in Great Britain
by Amazon

56776878R00139